ZOMBIE FLOCK

Zombie Flock

A NOVEL BY

CLARA VOLAR

For Tecia

Chapter 1 – Hatchling Bacteria

Harold sat beside Margaret and listened to her moan. The pain had begun an hour after she had worked in the rose garden weeding and tending to her petaled beauties. She groaned and Harold rearranged her blanket so that it covered her shoulders and offered her another pain-killer, which she gladly took. He had never seen her in so much pain nor had he felt so helpless. Although he was a scientist, an ornithologist, in fact, he knew little of medicine and understood her pain was beyond anything he could manage.

He carried her fevered body to the car and gingerly placed her in the passenger's seat, careful to fasten her seatbelt. He ran to the driver's side, dropped his keys and clumsily scooped them up before opening his door, scooting into his seat and cramming the keys into the ignition. As the engine bucked to life he pulled out of the driveway and raced towards the hospital as quickly as he could in L.A. traffic.

Margaret had been with him since high school and twenty years beyond that; she had been his only love and now she was practically catatonic as she slumped beside him. Harold gently reached for her with his right hand and found her skin to be hotter than he imagined possible for a human. A grand mal seizure took control of her; she convulsed beside him, arms flailing, head whipping back and forth, rocking their small car as it crept through traffic. "Margaret, Margaret!" he screamed with a voice that sounded far more like an ambulance siren than the sounds he had produced all his life. His thoughts bounced through his head, too random and horrific to analyze or use to formulate a plan. Her body lurched forward as she projectile vomited copious amounts of blood onto the dashboard. With a final convulsion she went rigid, her head cocked to the side and she tipped towards the door, sightless eyes rolled back in their sockets. She was dead. A ringlet of curly brown hair slowly slid down her forehead and covered one of her hazel-green eyes.

Through all the honking, and blatant anger of the rush-hour drivers, Harold managed to pull over to the far right lane. "Margaret, no, please no," he whispered hoarsely. He pulled her towards him, the silence of the car bearing down on him, her limp body already feeling forcign. His hazard lights blinked in time with his rapid breathing. It couldn't be possible, not his Margaret. Just hours before he could hear her singing in the garden and could see her pause to admire the countless birds that frequented their feeders.

He reached into his pocket and retrieved his phone. Shaking and bewildered, he dialed emergency assistance. He had always thought of himself as stoic and pragmatic, but the call he placed was barely understandable as he blubbered to the woman on the other end. "Please help. I can't. . ., I don't know what to do! Margaret isn't breathing. I'm pulled over on the freeway hoping, just hoping there's someone who can save her." Within minutes emergency vehicles surrounded his Prius.

What was it he had heard about a crisis? That time moves in a different rhythm, that events seemed to slow down or swirl around in a dreamlike fashion. At this moment, a time he had never anticipated, there was nothing hazy or unreal; he saw each detail as clearly as the specimens he studied under the microscope each day at the research lab. Leaning against his car in the brilliant sunlight, Harold pushed his glasses up to the proper resting place on his nose and stared at the badge of the highway patrolman who was questioning him. If he tilted his head to the right a brilliant light gleamed from its metal and seemed to sparkle like a star on a clear night.

The officer cleared his throat, "Mr. Harbinger. I'm Officer Bill Stetson. Would you like me to escort you to the hospital or would you prefer to come in my vehicle?"

Harold studied the man's face, it betrayed no emotion; clearly this was not the first time he had marched through this protocol. His eyes were a soft blue, almost childlike with their innocence and his skin was smooth and soft, freshly shaved. The patrolman smelled of coffee and Harold let the old cliché channel through his thoughts and wondered if a donut was currently digesting along with the cup of Joe in the officer's stomach.

"Mr. Harbinger?" he stated once again, but only received the same result. Harold might have seen the setting clearly, but Margaret's violent death had rendered him speechless.

--

Paramedics had Margaret on a stretcher complete with a white sheet covering her every inch. They worked fluidly as a team and effortlessly hoisted her body into the back of the ambulance. Chuck backed into the vehicle pulling the gurney and its rider in with him, David lifted from the opposite end. They worked smoothly together and had done so for three years, little had to be said between them as they both understood that there was nothing to be done with the woman other than transport her to the hospital for a look see before the inevitable autopsy to determine the cause of death. As Chuck stepped deeper into the ambulance the sheet caught on equipment and was pulled from the woman's face, revealing rose-colored spots on her cheeks and forehead.

Chuck leaned closer, studying the blotches with interest. "I just read about that in my textbook, the spots are called Horder's spots," he said with confidence.

David was proud of his friend for taking on classes yet again that would move him towards medical school, but he also felt the pinch of jealousy. "Hey, Mr. Big Shot, let's leave the diagnosing to the real doctors."

Chuck ignored him and leaned forward to tidy the sheet and cover the woman's face and return the respect he felt all dead deserved. As he covered her face Chuck thought he saw her eyes move beneath the lids just before the sheet settled into place and he sprang back.

David was startled by his movements and turned to stare at his friend. "What's the matter, did ya see a ghost," he asked before grabbing onto the armrest and preparing to settle into his chair. Chuck's mouth hung open as he took a step back. David almost laughed out loud, but he knew Chuck was no sissy and there must have been a good reason for his reaction.

Chuck dug his hands into his hips and took his "I'll prove I'm right" pose. "You go ahead and get a look at her then. Go, right on up close and check out her eyes," Chuck hurled the words at his friend with more sourness than he intended; fear altered his speech.

Up front the engine of the ambulance sounded and Stan eased the car into drive. David continued to secure his seat. Chuck sat near him but continued to glare. "Go ahead now, lift the sheet," he said with more calm coating his words.

"Come on man, this isn't funny," David said as he looked at the gurney.

Chuck nudged him, "Do it!"

David had grown up with three brothers and had learned the hard way over the years what could happen if you did not man up and take the dare. He hadn't realized he was holding his breath until he felt his chest relax as a loud gust of air burst free. "Fine, I'll take a peek." Reluctantly, he unfastened his seat belt.

He tucked his beach-blonde hair behind one ear and leaned forward. He took one last look at Chuck before lifting the sheet. Sure he had watched his share of horror movies and had made his quota of comments out loud like, *Don't go outside stupid,* or better yet, *Turn on the lights!* There was a horror movie quality to the moment that almost made him laugh. How could he possibly be afraid of a dead woman? The phrase that sprinted into his thoughts was, *Don't take the sheet off idiot!* He looked at Chuck and they were so full of emotion all they could do was share a nervous laugh. They had been known to have laugh attacks as a result of high emotion and it appeared they were about to be taken over once again by a laughing session. Chuck's chuckle turned into a rumble deeper inside before it broke free and filled the inside of the ambulance with a cackling sort of full laugh.

David smiled at him, his bright eyes ablaze with youth and adventure. He leaned forward to lift the sheet, but moments before he reached the cloth the body bolted upright and dove at him, fingers clawing outward and digging straight into his eyes. He screamed as the long nails continued their journey down his face. Blinded and gagging with terror, he felt a lightning bolt of pain in his lower lip and heard a ripping sound as Chuck shrieked behind him. David's lower lip and most of the skin covering his chin disappeared into Margaret's mouth as she gobbled it hungrily. David's perfect, straight, white teeth that his mother had spent over $5,000 to straighten when he was fourteen were revealed for all to see.

Chuck had been too terror-stricken to move, but seeing his friend thrashing on the floor motivated him to take action. He reached on the shelf beside him, pulled a hypodermic needle from its wrapper, loaded it with a heavy sedative and crammed it into the woman's leg and shoved the plunger down. Rather than shut down as he hoped, she turned her vengeance on him. He punched her as hard as he could in the face, but she kept coming, fingers curling claw-like and seeking his eyes. He wrapped his hands around her wrists, but she pushed forward ramming her head into his, knocking his skull so hard it hit the window behind him. With Chuck temporarily immobilized, she took full advantage of her moment and dug deeply into his eyes.

Blood splattered the walls, Chuck and David fought together, sightless, and terrified beyond reality; both men had wet themselves. Chuck staggered towards the defibrillator that could send an electrical current through her heart and blast her back to hell from where she had sprung. His hands found the equipment and easily switched on the charger, but her attacks were feral and relentless. They battled until one at a time she discovered their jugulars and tore into them.

--

The ambulance siren blared above and Stan had his ear buds in and was listening to his favorite chill wave music, oblivious of the carnage occurring behind him. It was not until he saw, from the corner of his eye, that the glass separating them was spattered with blood that he pulled over. He turned to get a better look into the back of the ambulance where everything should have been serene and still. Both his buddies, the men who had called him "Stan the Man" were contorted, bloodied and still. As an ambulance driver he had seen more than his share of gore, but knowing the pulpy remains were his friends had an ungodly affect upon him. His vomiting began before he knew what to do. The first blast covered the steering wheel, the second splattered the trash-strewn grass on the side of the freeway as he flung open the door. He crouched low and wretched, his sounds reminding him of a sick seal. He vomited until nothing was left. When his strength returned he staggered to the back of the vehicle and found both doors open wide for the entire world to see Chuck and David without eyes, with chunks of flesh torn from their faces and worst of all, without dignity. Stan was able to radio for backup before he lost consciousness.

--

Harold leaned against the guardrail, unwilling to budge, unable to walk. The officer wrapped his arm securely around Harold's waist and urged him towards the cruiser. "You'll feel better after we get to the hospital and a doctor can take a look at you too. Come on now sir, everything is gunna to be just fine," he said with as much sincerity as he could muster.

Harold wiped the sweat from his brow and smoothed back his thick, black hair. "I'm not going anywhere without Margaret."

The officer softened his voice, which made him sound almost patronizing, "Sir, she is already in the ambulance on her way to the hospital. I'm going to take you to her in my car."

Harold's mouth was so dry he wondered how on such a scorching summer day when his body was drenched with sweat that his mouth could be so parched. He hoped Margaret wasn't thirsty too. "Could I please have two bottles of cold water," he asked. "Officer, she must be awfully thirsty by now and she does love a good cold drink of water."

"I tell you what. First of all, how about you call me Bill. Second of all, I'll get a nice cold drink for you at the hospital, but you have to get in the car first," Stetson spoke with as much tenderness as possible.

Harold's cognitive functioning had shut down. With no better options in front of him, he followed Officer Stetson to his car. Even before they reached the vehicle, crackling sounds from distress calls could be heard from dispatch loud and clear. "Emergency workers in trouble, officers and emergency personnel in close proximity are required on the scene. Any officer near Route 134 and near the exit of Forest Lawn Drive report to the premises immediately."

It wasn't standard procedure, but Officer Stetson had to head in that direction to get Mr. Harbinger to the hospital where his wife's dead body awaited. He thought he would get a look at the situation and see if it was worth his time to stop. Officer Stetson managed a weak smile, "Strap in Mr. Harbinger, we're about to put the pedal to the metal."

He switched on his lights and siren and headed towards the 134 and whatever tragedy had sprouted there since he last drove through the area. He arrived at the scene much sooner than he anticipated and was stunned to find the very ambulance that had toted Mrs. Harbinger pulled off the side of the road. Police and emergency vehicles parked and swarmed near the area. He pulled over to get a better look and was horrified to see two gurneys being taken from the ambulance and put into another. He felt fear take a toll on his body as his bowels began to rumble. "You stay put Mr. Harbinger and I'm gunna take a look see at this situation," he said without daring to get eye contact. If he was lucky Harold Harbinger was clueless and didn't realize it was the identical ambulance his wife had originally been placed in for her pointless journey to the hospital.

Within seconds of leaving his car he spotted Stan, known to all law enforcement as Stan the Man, sitting inside the tail end of an ambulance with a blanket wrapped around his shoulders. His eyes sought more clues as his mind tried to determine why on a hot July day a man would be draped in a blanket. The only plausible answer came to him in a snap – Stan was suffering from shock and must have been dragged through some type of hell before they got to him.

Bill quickened his steps sending gravel spiraling in all directions as he pounded the blacktop. It didn't seem he could walk fast enough to close the distance between himself and Stan. When he reached his friend, who was as pale as a cotton ball, draped in a brown blanket, and an IV taped into place in a large vein in his arm, he was barely recognizable. Officer Stetson nudged his way in and sat beside Stan inside the ambulance. Stan's brown eyes were focused on the ground, but he didn't appear to be aware of his surroundings. Bill wrapped his arm around Stan's shoulders, "Hey, Buddy, looks like you've been to hell and back. Wanna tell me what happened here?"

Stan looked at him, trembling and on the verge of tears. He hiccupped once as he tried to hold back the sobbing that lay beneath his façade.

The officer officially on duty approached and glared at him, deep groves forming between his brows showing his displeasure and his lips tucked down in a frown causing perfect half circles to form at the edges. "This is my case and I've everything under control, we don't need you here interfering."

"Look, officer, Stan and I go way back and I'm here to help a friend. Besides, less than half an hour ago I was with him as they loaded Mrs. Harbinger into his ambulance and set out for the hospital."

This final tidbit of information was Stetson's ticket into the circle of officers and the ongoing crisis. The officer relaxed his face and reached out his hand in a gesture of camaraderie. "Officer Johnson at your service." Both men shared grim smiles and exchanged what information they had.

Officer Johnson shook his head, "It's the damndest thing, both emergency workers were chewed on from the chest up. Looked like a coyote or mountain lion got into the ambulance and had its way with them. Chuck was barely alive when I first arrived on the scene, but he has since expired. He was so bad off he wasn't able to tell me anything." The underlying insinuation both understood was that Stan had not done his job properly; he was not "the Man" after all.

Bill was quick to question the obvious, "I saw two gurneys being carried out, what about Mrs. Harbinger, where is she?"

Officer Johnson stroked his chin and scratched the back of his head. "Damned if I know. Besides the driver and Chuck and David, the ambulance was empty. Her gurney was coated in blood, but she's gone."

Stetson looked around quickly to make sure Mr. Harbinger was still in the car and blissfully unaware of his wife's disappearance. At that moment, Mr. Harbinger rolled down his window and shouted, "How about that water? I could sure use a drink right now." Bill and Officer Johnson exchanged looks.

"That would be the deceased's spouse; he's a bit out of his mind right now and could use a cold drink." Without pausing, Bill grabbed a paper cup from the dispenser and filled it to the brim from the water container inside the ambulance. He was rattled by all that had transpired, mostly by the disappearance of Margaret Harbinger and the thoughts that she too had been torn to bits. However, he did his best to keep his hands from shaking as he carried the water to Harold Harbinger.

--

Darkness settled quietly over the landscape, emergency vehicles returned to their appropriate posts for the evening, but there would be little rest for the countless officers and rescue workers who had a glimpse of the horror. There were too many questions left unanswered. To begin with, where was Margaret Harbinger? There were no signs that her body had been drug from the scene by a wild animal, no tire tracks to suggest a human had arrived on the scene and toted her body away for God knew what reason. And, finally, what had happened to men who had sworn to save lives, but had lost their own instead.

--

On his fifth cup of coffee, Bill Stetson typed his report the best he could. He had watched as the doctor gave Mr. Harbinger a sedative, had personally taken him home, and left feeling that at least one person would sleep this night. There were so many blanks that remained in the telling of the events and in filling out the required paperwork. Bill picked up the phone to call the hospital, but put it back in its stand; it was far too soon for any autopsy results from the hospital. He pulled Officer Johnson's card from his pocket and turned it round and around in his fingers toying with the idea of calling him just in case he had any fresh news.

Stetson should have clocked out hours before, but he felt personally attached to this case and so rattled he wondered if he could fall asleep even if he went home. Ever since his wife left and the cat died, there didn't seem to be a reason to go home anyway. He drummed his fingers on the desk and went through the details of the day once again, one at a time, but nothing added up. After all his training and experience in the field not one thing had prepared him for the morbidity of this day.

Chapter 2 – Down Hill

Forest Lawn Cemetery was famous in California and adjoining states for the unmatchable beauty of its grounds. The rolling hills, intricate flowerbeds and towering trees were remarkable on their own, but the ornate statutes and fountains surrounding the ponds at the entrances both in Burbank and in Glendale, were picture worthy. Many a tourist had stopped to take photos of the legendary burial grounds.

Some mornings the mist was so thick the cemetery seemed a magical place and Miguel found that his favorite time to arrive at work was just before dawn and the other workers arrived. At this bewitching hour he could mount his lawnmower and move across the grounds, grooming the grass and doing his part to keep the magic of the scenery in place. He found the setting more comforting still when it was so early even the Mexicans selling bouquets of flowers on the roadside hadn't begun to set up for the day.

Because it was a chilly morning, even for July, Miguel brought a thermos of coffee and wore an extra layer to keep the cold from sinking into his bones. His mother had always told him that he had a sixth sense, a way of sensing the super natural or events yet to occur. He disregarded her insights as she was from old Mexico and still believed in the ancient superstitions. He was fairly certain she still believed in chupacabras, the infamous "goat suckers" as well. The chill continued to sink deeper within him despite the extra clothing and hot drink. Sixth sense or not, he brushed his concerns to the corner of his mind and focused on the job at hand – mowing the never-ending lawn.

He fired up the engine and began his first straight line right up the front lawn heading deeper into the cemetery grounds. The mist clung to him and in a small way, with its familiarity, it comforted him. As he crested the hill he looked to his right to take in the beauty of his favorite tree. It towered above the rest and appeared to protect all that slept their final slumber beneath the sod, dirt and roots. As he got closer and the fog did not obscure his view nearly as much, he spied the largest turkey vulture he had ever seen. It was hunched over, legs locked in roost mode on a thick branch and head tucked down beneath a wing. Although his machine continued to move forward he took a moment to look back and think how odd it was to see a solitary bird when they usually roosted in a cluster in the bigger trees.

Miguel finished his first perfectly even swatch up the grass just as the sun was starting to nibble at the sky and turned his machine around to head down the hill making a matching blaze of cut grass right beside his first. As he approached his beloved tree he noted that the buzzard was gone from the branch. That in itself was odd as the birds usually spread out their wings, took in the warmth of the sun, recharged their batteries and slowly began the day. He tugged his zipper higher on his neck and shuddered.

In his home country of Mexico, a lone bird was an omen of bad luck, a turkey vulture was even more so. Miguel knew his boss would arrive soon and he didn't take any crap from his workers especially when it came to all things superstitious. Miguel kept his eyes forward, passed the tree and continued down the hill intent on making the straightest line possible. Just one swatch of grass at a time and he would get through this day. Near the bottom on the hill as he approached the turnaround point, Miguel heard only the whir of the blades from the machine he rode, but he saw a large object dart to his left. He turned to get a better look, but whatever it was either disappeared behind his mower or hadn't been there to begin with.

He felt a small bump and thought he had run over a rock, but when he felt the icy cold fingers on his forehead all coherent thoughts fled from his mind. He screamed, screamed the way he had heard women let loose in horror films. He shrieked louder as a face with wild curly hair and a bloody mouth appeared beside him. She shrieked like a bird and raised her sharp fingers intent on clawing into his eyes. He jerked his head to the left, but she caught one eye and dug in deep. He felt a searing pain and heard a popping sound and knew his right eye had been dug from his face. Without a second thought he brought up the heavy thermos and slammed it into the woman's head. Caught by surprise, she tried to grab onto him, but his jacket was slick from the morning mist, she lost her grip and tumbled backwards off the mower.

Miguel shifted gears on his machine and pushed it to its speed limit. He began mumbling a prayer and crying, tears coursing down his left check. He knew he had to focus on putting distance between them, but reached up to wipe something moist from his right cheek. The goo that had once been his right eye, looking very much like undercooked egg white mixed with chocolate, squished between his fingers. "God help me! Help me!" Miguel screamed even though there was nobody near to help. He glanced quickly behind him and she was catching up, not exactly running, it was more of a stagger, but still she was coming at him looking crazed and determined to kill.

He saw the pond and fountains below and wondered if he made it to the water and climbed the statue, maybe, just maybe, she wouldn't be able to swim and he could escape. One more look behind and he realized he wouldn't make it to the fountain in time. He steered with his left hand and took a firm hold of his thermos with his right. He had always been an excellent batter in baseball and, if she was lucky enough to climb up again, he planned to knock her head in and fling her off his machine by God.

She lumbered along, at times faster than others, reaching out and trying to grab hold of the mower. Miguel knew full well she would tear him to bits if she could, why she wanted to he couldn't fathom, but he knew it with certainty. The back end of his machine bounced down as she jumped onto it. He understood that the terrifying moment he had dreaded was finally here. She wailed and jumped onto his back, with one fluid movement he swung the thermos behind his head and made solid contact with her skull. She uttered a guttural cawing sound and slumped backwards. As his machine moved forward, he turned and brought the thermos down straight into her face. Blood and fragments of bone shot from her nose, or what had once been her nose. He turned long enough to slam on the brakes, put the mower in neutral and shove her off.

When he heard her body plop onto the ground he wound up the engine again to its fastest speed, turned the mower around and charged at his target while she squirmed on the ground. He hit her feet first and the mower struggled to take on such bulky objects, but within a few seconds it had gobbled up her toes and started the process of pulverizing her feet. The blades did their job well and then caught her black, peasant skirt and began to mulch it. The mower was the best on the market and the blades were sturdy and sharp, but for this morning they had taken on all they could. The lawnmower could not go further, but either could the crazed woman beneath it.

Miguel turned off his machine, climbed down, but stayed a safe distance. Pinned beneath, writhing and squawking was a woman with the craziest face and hair he had ever seen. How she was still alive he wasn't sure, but he knew enough to stay far away from her. With hands that were surprisingly still, he pulled out his cell phone, flipped open the cover and stared at the blurry numbers. Obviously, he had not gotten used to seeing with only one eye. As he focused on the buttons and aimed, a brilliant, ruby-colored droplet fell from his empty eye socked, splattered onto number nine, showing him the way, the first number to push that would bring help. He finished with the following one, one with little difficulty.

Chapter 3 – Like a Rooster With its Head Cut Off

Bill Stetson had been up all night and had been listening to the police radio and was the first to arrive on the scene. When he saw that it was indeed Mrs. Harbinger beneath the mower and that she was in fact alive, he sat right down on the grass. It was his turn to be speechless. As the ambulance arrived and the emergency workers began treating Miguel the question that sat center stage in Stetson's mind was how? How was she alive, how did she get out of the ambulance and what in the world went wrong at the cemetery. How did an employee accidentally hit a woman on foot?

His pants were damp from the grass and he felt like a damn fool for sitting down to begin with and eased himself back up onto his feet. Officers started swarming around Miguel as well as his boss all wanting to know what happened. Stetson was on the periphery of the conversation and only heard snippets of the interrogation. "Do you want an attorney present at the hospital?"

From what he could gather, this Miguel fellow didn't want an attorney he wanted someone to deal with the woman under his mower, wanted the insanity to stop and just wanted to mow the lawn. His boss was adamant that proper protocol was followed and that the police were allowed to do their jobs.

As the emergency workers approached the mower Miguel called out to them. "I wouldn't go near her if I was you." The two men looked at each other and kept walking. "Hey, this is no joke man!" Miguel said with as much force as he could muster. "She tried to kill me and she would've if I hadn't run her over." All three of them looked down and at the same moment and noticed hacked off pieces of her feet, toes and shredded cloth on the grass directly behind the mower, each wondering what else had been severed by the efficient steel blades.

Stetson came up to them for a better look and he too noticed the hacked bits of flesh and the detached digits, saw them clearly enough to notice the purple nail polish. "How am I gunna tell Mr. Harbinger about this?" The three men looked at him as if he had lost his mind, which he probably had considering the circumstances.

Stetson walked over to the ambulance, removed his hat and looked at Miguel. His eye was patched and they were preparing him to go to the hospital, but there was so much Stetson had to know. "Do you mind if I ask you some questions, Miguel?"

An emergency worker looked at him crossly, "We have to get him to the hospital. You can take his statement later."

Stetson persisted, "I understand, but could you at least tell me where she came from?"

Miguel broke down and started sobbing softly. He wiped his nose with his sleeve. "She came from a tree."

--

After Miguel was on his way to the hospital in the first ambulance, the emergency workers stepped forward.

"We need to do something for that poor woman, crazy or not. We can't leave her under there."

The maintenance manager of the cemetery had arrived and agreed to help the EMTs. It took him no time at all to start the engine, put it in reverse and begin the process of backing the machine off the woman. Each inch the mower moved it dragged the lady with it, which made it necessary for the medical team to take hold of her and pull from their end while the machine went the opposite direction. Fortunately, they had thought to wear gloves and had on long sleeves so her attempts to claw at them were futile. They held her arms and pulled while the machine backed away. To call what remained of her legs grizzled would be an understatement. There were no feet, only sharp angles of bone protruding from just below the knees. Tendons, muscle and bits of her black skirt stuck to what remained of her lower limbs.

Freed from the mower, she began to kick with all her might, her gnarled stumps pumping wildly trying to knock over the men surrounding her. Droplets of blood and bodily fluids became airborne and spattered the white clothing of the workers. Gerald, the EMT wearing John Lennon glasses, was most bothered by the crimson droplets as they kept landing on the lenses and obscuring his vision.

Stetson took an immediate dislike to him. Bill had been a child of the 60s and had grown up loving the Beatles, but in the year 2013 seeing a grown man in Lennon specs brought about a feeling that the wearer was more weasel than man. *Punk*, thought Stetson to himself.

"Get the hypo and knock this bitch out!" growled Gerald.

His boss, Thomas, looked at him crossly. "She's a victim, not a bitch, Gerald, and we're here to help so watch your mouth."

The third member of the emergency team, Herman, had short, brown, military style hair and seemed like the responsible member of the trio. He ran back to the ambulance and returned with a syringe filled with clear liquid. He looked perplexed like a child who can't quite get the building blocks to stack just right. "How're we supposed to give her this while she is thrashing around so much?"

Thomas had little patience for Herman to begin with and was already on the verge of firing both his subordinates when he decided it was time to step in and show them how it was done. "Hold her arms and give me some room boys while I pin her legs."

Stetson watched with intrigue and fright thinking the entire scene looked like it sprang from a bad zombie movie and knowing these men had no idea what they were dealing with. He stared as Thomas straddled her, put his full weight on her thighs and then administered the sedative into her neck. The moment he pulled the needle out of her vein Gerald and Herman expected the usual total unconsciousness, relaxed and released her arms. Margaret's head rolled to the side and Thomas sat back on his heels.

Margaret shot forward faster than a rooster in a fighting arena and clawed into Thomas's lovely, green eyes.

The three men surrounding him shrieked in unison and his employees dove forward to help. Herman tried to recapture her arms, but she was a blur of clawing, flailing nails and gnawing teeth, snapping at arms and taking chunks of flesh, swallowing as she chewed. Gerald kicked her in the ribs and hollered for help. Bill Stetson alone had the presence of mind to put her down for good. Working by instinct and academy training, he pulled his pistol from its holster, clicked off the safety and blasted Margaret Harbinger in the head.

Her skull hit the grass with a mighty thunk, her milky grey eyes facing the heavens, not seeing a flock of crows as they flew overhead.

Chapter 4 – Suspension

Bill Stetson was suspended with pay until an extensive investigation could be conducted. He was told to stay clear of Mr. Harbinger, his home and to completely step out of the case and leave it to the police. He was a man's man, but shame was all he could feel and he questioned each step he had taken at the cemetery over and over in his mind. *What if?* seemed to be the theme in his brain for the morning.

His boss, Dick Townsend, toyed with the waddle beneath his chin and narrowed his eyes. "Did you really have to shoot her for God's sake?" he questioned, "She only had half her legs."

Stetson had already asked himself that several times before, but hearing the words out loud made his stomach clench. He saw her ravaged body all over again, saw the wild hair flying as she clawed and gnashed at the EMTs. He felt the gun in his hands and heard the blast. At that moment he thought he deserved to be fired not suspended.

"She was rippin' them to shreds. Take their full statements and find out for yourself," Stetson retorted with enough vinegar to finish the questioning.

Dick's glare continued. "I'm making a stop at the hospital later to see how those EMTs are doing," he said. "I hear one will need a complete face transplant, like that's gunna happen any time soon." Dick gave him a parting shot. "You stay away from them you hear, you've done enough harm already."

The last comment was infuriating; Stetson had saved all three of them. If he hadn't used his handy pistol, there would be three more dead medics to mourn.

Bill was certain he had to personally visit Harold Harbinger, but exactly what he would say to explain shooting Margaret he had no clue. The entire scene that played out at the cemetery seemed like a bad grade B science fiction movie. But, he had been the one to shoot her, he had been the one to make it final and official. He had never been eloquent and assumed he wouldn't be able to console Harbinger, but he had to try.

--

Guilt squeezed his whole being as if a paramedic had wrapped him in gauze and secured it too tightly. It was hard to breathe, harder still to think of what he had done and the mushed remains of what had been Margaret Harbinger. But he knew he had to get to Harold and share the grizzly news before another officer, perhaps one with a cold personality, delivered the word first. It was a responsibility he adopted and one he felt he owed Harold. He could even face serious reprimands by his superior officer if he was caught at the Harbinger home, but he had to risk it.

He rang the Harbinger doorbell and heard the shuffling of feet as Harold made his way to the door. He peeked through the slit in the door held in place by the security chain and ran his fingers through his hair. No amount of grooming, short of a shower and a good combing, could restore Harold's hair to orderly. It stood up in spiky bunches across his scalp and reminded Bill of the cock named Samson that ruled the henhouse when he was a boy on a farm and chickens scurried around his parent's property.

Harold squinted at him through the bright morning light that peeked through the front door around him. Still not recognizing the officer, he cleared his throat, "Could I help you?"

Bill removed his hat unveiling his salt and pepper hair and proceeded to explain himself, but was caught off guard by a coarse voice shouting from the kitchen. "Margaret, I'm home! Margaret, I'm home!"

On it went until Harold called into the kitchen, "Time to stop now Plato." Stetson heard a mumbled version of the same words echoing from the back area of the home he assumed was the kitchen. "Time to stop now Plato."

Harold looked over his shoulder and uttered a quick explanation, "It's my parrot, Plato. He's an African Grey and quite prolific." Harbinger finally recognized Stetson as the man who had spent the better part of the day with him the day before and eased the chain from the door.

Stetson cleared his throat and eased inside the door without being invited. "Mr. Harbinger, I have come with some news about Margaret."

Harold looked at him, hope slowly appearing on his face. "Where is she, is she okay, can I speak with her?"

"Mr. Harbinger, I'm so sorry, but yesterday when she was taken from you and put in the ambulance she had already passed on," he explained. "What transpired in the ambulance I have no idea because both EMTs with her died, but she was found on the grass of Forest Lawn Cemetery this morning." Stetson explained more of the drama that had unfolded before his eyes and that he had actually been the one to shoot her. He could not look Harold in the face any longer. "She is most certainly dead and an officer of the law will arrive shortly to give you more details."

"Margaret, I'm Home!" resounded from the back room.

"But, but. . . I was certain somehow they were wrong and she was alive because she wasn't in the ambulance any longer," stammered Harold. "Nothing you're saying makes any sense, you wouldn't shoot Margaret, you're the man who was helping us yesterday."

Stetson put his hand on Harbinger's shoulder. "Harold, may I call you Harold?"

Harbinger nodded in agreement. Whatever tears he had not shed during the night began to slip silently down his cheeks. Stetson guessed there were still gallons left unshed.

"She most certainly has passed on. But, I wanted to give you my card and let you know I'm here if you need me in any way. I'm so very sorry for your loss, I really am. I wouldn't have, you know . . . I had to she was killing those men." Stetson swallowed and gave Harold a few moments for the information to sink in. "Please call if you need anything." Stetson handed him his card and turned to leave. As he took the first step out the door he heard a sweeter, higher, more lady-like voice call from the back "See you soon."

Bill looked over his shoulder and Harold gave a sad little smile. "He can sound just like Margaret too and those were her parting words for every visitor who left our home."

Chapter 5 – With a Bird's Eye View

Later that day, early afternoon, alone in the morgue Harold looked down on his wife's remains. She had been such a beauty when they met twenty something years before with her curly brown hair, a few golden brown spirals lightened by the sun at her temples and all of it shiny with youth. Her lips had been full and quick to smile, especially when they were working together in the field studying birds. For both of them birds were the most magical creatures on the planet. Margaret had explained it simply once, "What other animals can sing and fly?" In their estimation, other facts such as their ability to navigate thousands of miles to migrate and to create nests without ever having been shown how to do so, raised birds to the highest pedestal possible. Harold had never thought in his lifetime he would meet another human who loved birds as much as he did, but Margaret and he had been of one heart and mind when it came to birds and it did not take long for them to fall in love with each other as well.

As he looked down at the body they claimed was his wife he could barely believe it. The right side of her head had a huge hollow from where the bullet entered, her face was covered with swirly red patches, her nose was smashed in, dirt and bits of twigs and leaves were wound throughout her hair and blood coated her lower face. He lifted the sheet to see what else had become of her body. The officer with him stepped closer, "Sir, make sure you do not touch or remove anything as the investigation is ongoing."

Harold wanted to shove him aside and have his time with Margaret. Harold raised his voice and looked the officer straight in the eye. "You say this is my wife, my wife! It doesn't look a thing like her."

The officer lowered his eyes, "Sir, I told you it wasn't a good idea to come in here and see her this way."

"Get out of here and let me be with her alone. Damn your investigation, I need time with her," Harold screamed, tears not far behind his words.

Human compassion stirred within the officer. "Sir, I'll give you five minutes, then I have to come back in, I'm under orders."

When Harold saw the bloody nails and hands he was disgusted, but there was no question as to who this woman was as her wedding ring, the very one they had chosen together, was sparkling on her left ring finger. He stared at it, ignoring the gore and blood beneath her fingernails. He raised her hand and kissed it gently before placing it back beneath the sheet.

The Horder's spots on her cheeks drew his attention and helped him focus his thoughts in the direction of science in search of why Margaret had gotten so ill and died. He thought back to the afternoon from the day before and found it hard to believe just yesterday she had been alive. His clues such as her high fever, were starting to formulate a hypothesis, but without a tissue sample he was lost. He looked behind him and saw the officer standing near the door, his back to Harold, blocking anyone from entering. Without a second thought, Harold removed a vial from his pocket and a swab. He swiped inside her nose, gently moving aside bone fragments, and pushed the swab as deep as possible to reach membranes that would hold bacteria. With the sample gathered, it took only seconds to place the swab inside the tube and cap it. Just as he slid the vial into his pocket, the officer came back into the room and announced that it was time to leave.

Harold put both hands gently on Margaret's hair and tried to smooth her curls, but it was so matted and full of debris it did no good.

"Sir, you really must leave now. As soon as the investigation is complete there will be more time before the burial."

--

Harold and Margaret had tried unsuccessfully for years to have children. In the end they decided to hand-feed a baby African Grey parrot to see if they could not only help the bird create a massive vocabulary, but also to see if it was possible to teach him to have human characteristics. For all intents and purposes Plato the parrot was their child. He could speak over two hundred words, could sort colors, do basic addition, and understood simple commands such as time for bed or put your toys away.

During the day Plato was in the kitchen area on a play stand where he could see and hear all that went on. Just as many parrots did, he could perfectly imitate the ringing of the home phone as well as each different ring tone for both cells. He knew their morning greetings, could make a kissing sound that always made them smile and reach forward to plant a kiss on his beak, his black tongue gently kissing them in return.

Harold had never been good at making friends and his parents had died years before. He went home from the morgue that day feeling emptier than he had ever known and sought the company of his only real friend. As soon as he entered the door Plato shouted, "Margaret, I'm home!" Harold dropped to his knees and rolled into a fetal position and let the sobs and tears tumble out of him. What must have been hours later he awoke right where he had landed and slowly eased himself upright, noting his creaky knees and feeling that he was no longer a young man.

Plato was grumbling and making his angry sounds. Harold heard him pick up his food bowl and drop it and as he heard Harold's steps grow closer he made a shrill whistle, Harold's least favorite sound, and announced "Dinner!" In the depths of his despair and confusion Harold had left home that day without feeding Plato and now it was late afternoon, no wonder the bird was angry.

Harold went into the bedroom, opened the cage door, mumbled an apology and reached for his friend. Plato's eyes were dilating as he studied Harold's face. He could always read their emotions and within moments his anger turned to empathy. Rather than nip at Harold he stepped gingerly onto his outstretched hand and leaned forward to cuddle against Harold's neck. Harold wrapped his arms around him and rocked him like he was a baby; it was a favorite pastime for both of them ever since Plato was tiny and just sprouting his grey, fluffy feathers.

Together they made their way into the kitchen where Harold scrambled to get Plato's favorite foods from the fridge and cupboard. He sliced grapes as Plato reached down and plucked them up, gobbling them so quickly Harold could not cut fast enough. Then he put a handful of peanuts on the playpen and set Plato on his stand. Plato cracked open each peanut and crunched the contents as Harold leaned against the counter. "Drink please," Plato croaked.

Harold fished the jug of orange juice from the fridge and poured a small bowl for his pet. "Here, buddy. I'm so, so sorry."

Plato happily dipped his beak into the juice and tipped his head back each time so the juice could trickle down his throat. "Nanna," Plato bleated, and Harold pealed a fresh banana for him and handed it over and Plato quickly ate half of it and let the other side drop to the floor of his play stand.

Satisfied with his meal, Plato let a large dollop of dark green droppings plop to the floor of the playpen. Harold, forever the ornithologist, thought the droppings looked runny, but didn't think much more of it because at that moment he also he remembered the sample he had taken from Margaret that was still in his pocket. He wondered after all these hours if there was still anything to see, but the vial had remained in a warm place, his pocket, and bacteria thrived in tepid, moist environments.

While Harold set up his microscope on the kitchen counter and turned on more lights, Plato ran through his repertoire. "Love you, Buddy. Smart bird, here kitty, kitty, naughty birdie, help please, love you Harold, love you Harold, love you Harold," and finally, "Want scratch and play." Harold had completely set up the scope and the sample, but he was helpless when Plato used his sweetest voice and begged to be played with. African Greys are much like two-year-old children and know how to demand attention. Knowing what was coming, Plato jumped to the counter, rolled on his back and started putting one grey foot in the air and rolling side to side. Ten minutes after they had finished playing, Harold found he was smiling, a huge genuine grin and hugged the bird to him. It had been the first time since yesterday afternoon that Margaret had not dominated his thoughts or at least his subconscious. The bird snuggled in closer, "Love you, Harold."

Safe in his home, with a creature he adored and who loved him in return, Harold rocked Plato in his arms like he was a baby and allowed the tears and sobs to take over.

Chapter 6 – Psittacosis

The bacteria were clearly viewable under the scope, but Harold could not put a name to them. There was something so familiar about the circular forms that moved slowly within the mucous sample, but he couldn't identify them. True, he wasn't thinking as clearly as possible considering losing Margaret in such a horrible way, losing her twice in fact. He took off his glasses and rubbed his eyes; that particular mannerism used to annoy Margaret because she felt it introduced germs into his eyes, she was correct of course, and because she said it would cause premature wrinkling. He wiped his glasses clean with the end of his shirt and propped them back up on his nose.

The house was quiet except for the incessant practicing of Plato, but it was quiet enough for Harold to think back to almost twenty years before when he and his colleagues were studying speech capability in various parrots. A shipment had arrived fresh off the boat, as they say, and he and his co-workers were eager to start working with them to determine which species were most capable of acquiring speech or simple mimicry.

A week after the arrival of the birds all workers in the lab came down with symptoms that were similar to pneumonia as well as typhoid fever; they all had high fevers, diarrhea, rose spots on their faces and the worst headaches any of them had ever known. The supervisor of the research facility was furious when he found out that the birds brought into the lab had not gone through the customary isolation and testing period to make sure they were disease-free.

After the researchers had been hospitalized, quarantined and offered up countless tubes of blood, it was finally determined that the research team all had psittacosis also known as parrot fever. Fortunately for all of them it was treatable with tetracycline and chloramphenicol intravenously. Within 48-72 hours all their symptoms began to dissipate. Some team members, Harold included, had relapses and had to go through round two of antibiotics.

As Harold returned his attention to the microscope he realized the bacterium looked very much like C. psittaci, the very bacteria that had gotten all of them sick, but the circular bacteria were misshapen and clearly had mutated. Harold adjusted the instrument and took another long look; he was certain the bacteria was related to that found in parrot fever, but he had to verify his findings. He picked up the phone to call his boss but stopped before pushing the final button. He had heard the expression cold sweat before, and now he understood how it had been used so often it was considered a cliché because he was sweating profusely, felt chilled to the core and goose bumps were sprouting rapidly on his arms. It was one thought that had triggered this physical reaction, one thought so horrific he was afraid to let his brain follow the logical thread all the way to the end.

His conclusion was that if the bacteria scooped from Margaret's nasal passage was similar to the bacteria in psittacosis, then it was logical it came from Plato, who had contracted it from Harold himself somehow from his clothing or items he had brought home from the lab. He and a select team of ornithologists had been researching psittacosis for months in an attempt to find a vaccine to prevent the acquisition of the disease for birds and humans alike. They had taken every precaution, they thought, even wearing bio-hazard suits, to contain the bacteria and not let a single spore leave the building.

Contracting parrot fever, scientifically known as Chlamydophila psittaci, simplified as C. psittaci, was very easy, it only took breathing near bird droppings or their nasal secretions that contained the bacteria. This toxic microbe was easily airborne and could remain infectious for months.

Because bacteria were living, microscopic creatures looking for hosts in warm moist environments, it was logical to think perhaps Harold himself had the bacteria in his system, but for some reason he was immune, likely because he had been hit so hard by parrot fever twenty years ago and his body had built up a resistance. Without delay, Harold swabbed deep into his nasal cavity and smeared the findings on glass slides for viewing under the scope, but no bacteria resembling C. psittaci was present.

The sizeable blob of Plato's droppings were still moist in the middle and were easy enough to swab; they too contained the unnamed bacteria. He stared at Plato who was happily preening his feathers, reaching back every now and again to rub his beak on his preening gland to extract the precious feather dust that was a fine, white, waxy substance that kept his feathers waterproof and also contained an antibacterial property.

This powder also kept his feathers healthy and capable of flight and gave him a slightly sweet smell.

Harold was so stunned by Plato's obvious health and the presence of the bacteria in his system that he had to sit down. His brain focused on the present and he concentrated all his scientific training, experience with birds and education on the topic of "how." The obvious conclusion that surfaced was that Plato was a carrier of the bacteria, something of a Typhoid Mary; he could pass along the disease, but was not impacted by it.

Harold looked again at Plato. The bird had its head twisted sideways while his foot gingerly groomed around his eye lids. His white lids remained closed as one black claw carefully preened the tiny feathers near his eyelashes and beak. As if he knew he was being watched, he opened one pale yellow eye and stared right at Harold, startling him enough that Harold jumped in his seat. It was as if Plato was reading his mind.

Following the logical line of reasoning, Harold allowed his mind to make more conclusions. If Plato was a carrier of a deadly bacteria and had unknowingly given it to Margaret, he might also have shared his germs with the countless wild birds that ate under their feeders. Margaret used to love to work in the garden and while she weeded, pruned and planted Plato was her constant companion. He usually started out on his perch, but enjoyed wandering around the yard gathering sticks or peeking under rocks. He had even been known to snatch his share of seed from the feeders. If Harold was on the right track, Plato's bacteria, straight from Harold's lab, could be within the droppings in his yard.

He grabbed sample tubes and swabs and started out the backdoor. "Fresh air and sunshine time, Plato!" the bird called in his best Margaret voice. Harold stopped immediately and held onto the counter. Hearing Margaret, or at least Plato's version of her, was a physical pain in his gut. Harold stopped to take a deep breath and regroup. He took a large drink of water as Plato climbed to his shoulder and rubbed against his cheek until Harold shared the last swallows with him. Harold grabbed a handful of antacid tablets and chewed them quickly.

Plato stared up at the brilliant, blue sky and in Margaret's tones sang out, "Yep, another gorgeous day!" As soon as they were outside Harold placed the bird on his backyard play stand and walked towards the biggest feeder. A small flock of song birds and sparrows scattered in all directions, each chirping small distress calls. Under the feeder he found several moist samples and scooped them one at a time into vials.

Task complete, he tried to pick up Plato from the stand and onto his shoulder, but Plato would have none of it. "Yep, another gorgeous day, yep, another gorgeous day," he chanted. Harold knew this was Plato's attempt at more outdoor time, but today was not the day; there were too many important questions to answer. Plato nipped at him as he went to grab him again. Harold took a strong hold of Plato's beak between his thumb and forefinger and said angrily, "No! Inside now!"

The bird was not used to such harshness and tucked his head under his wing and mumbled. Harold hated it when he did that; it was like he was a naughty child talking back to his parents, but only as he was walking out of the room with his back turned so they could not hear the vulgarities he was saying to them.

As they approached the house Harold could hear the phone ringing. He didn't care if it was the President of the United States, he was not picking up until he had answers. Inside the house he could hear the tail-end of a voice message, someone he did not recognize asking him to please call right away. The message had barely clicked off when he felt the familiar vibration of his cell in his pocket. The temptation to answer was acute, but first he had to get the droppings onto the slides and then under the scope.

In less than ten minutes three of the four samples proved positive for the same bacteria that had been thriving inside Margaret. Harold's stomach felt like he had drunk battery acid for lunch. His worst fears had just been confirmed. Somehow he had brought home a bacteria with him, given it to his beloved pet who in turn gave it to Margaret. That was just the beginning of the problem; the wild birds were contaminated and as they ate, flew and defecated, they were spreading the bacteria to countless humans. He didn't know what the incubation period was or how long it took for symptoms to present themselves, the only thing he knew for sure was that residents of Southern California were in for an ungodly epidemic.

As the devastating reality of his part in spreading the bacteria and Margaret's death descending upon him, the doorbell rang. "For God's sake! What now?" grumbled Harold. From his view in the peep hole he could see a police officer. He thought that he was likely the person trying so desperately to reach him on the telephone. His first impulse was to remain silent and pretend he was not home.

"Mr. Harbinger, we have a serious problem and our department feels you might be the man to help us," the officer said in his most respectful tone. Harold watched as he removed his hat and wiped the sweat from his brow.

Harold's options were dwindling; he could remain in reclusion and denial, or he could open the door and tell the officer all he knew. Or, better still, he could tell him just enough to buy him time to try and find an antidote.

Harbinger unlatched the chain. He didn't even attempt a smile. "What exactly do you need from me officer?"

"Sir, let me introduce myself, I'm Police Chief Darren Ogden," he said. "There have been five more cases similar to yours, I mean, similar to what happened to Mrs. Harbinger, reported in the general area," he stated flatly. "Do you know anything about what might be causing these illnesses?"

"Margaret, I'm Home!" echoed from the kitchen. Ogden briefly glanced in that direction.

Harold held the door open wider and stepped aside, indicating the officer could enter. "Have a seat." Harold tucked all his emotions aside and focused on the logical and any way he could distract the officer. "Mr. Ogden, why in the world would I know what happened to Margaret or anyone else?"

"Sir, it's just that Mrs. Harbinger, well, witnesses say she moved like a bird," he said without losing eye contact. "Other witnesses say the people they saw with the sickness showed the exact movements."

Harold was confused. "When did Margaret move like a bird?"

"At the cemetery, when she attacked the gardener," he explained. "He used words like swooped, and claw-like fingers trying to gouge out his eyes. He also said she was perched in a tree." Townsend went on to explain that as each person had died from the identical illness and risen again, they had attacked with such ferocity and bird-like actions it was almost like a scene from the movie *Birds*.

Harold played ignorant. Plato shouted from the back room, "Margaret, I am home!"

"Mr. Harbinger, the obvious here is that you are an ornithologist, work with birds each day, apparently you have some type of parrot on the premises and your wife was the first taken with the disease and the first to attack," He scratched the back of his neck and stared deep into Harold's eyes. "What's going on here? If we don't find out soon a whole lot a people are gunna die and a lot more are going to get hurt."

Harbinger took a deep breath and let it out. "Look, my mind is all over the place right now. I'm heartsick about my wife, or don't you get that? She and I had a solid marriage, a special one and she died a horrible death." Harold stood and gestured towards the door. "I think you should leave."

"Sir, with all due respect, we can have a casual chat here, or we can go to the station," said Ogden with his hardened police chief voice. "I know you're hurting, but we're desperate here and need some help."

Harold turned his back, took off his glasses and rubbed his eyes again. He could feel the tears welling up behind his lids and he would be damned if he would let this officer see him cry. He steadied himself and turned back to the officer. "I may be onto something that is causing this, but I need time to find out."

"Mr. Harbinger, every minute that goes by more and more people are catching this nasty bug. Any help you can offer might just shut this down," Ogden frowned. "The bacteria they found in your wife's blood was like nothing we've seen before. The medical examiner said it was a total mystery to him."

Harold let out a long sigh and sat back down. "It's a long story, could I get you a cold drink?"

For the next half hour Harbinger described the research facility where he and his coworkers tried each day to find a vaccine for psittacosis, how they used bio hazard suits and that the bacteria was so powerful years back the U.S. Government actually attempted to harness it to use in chemical warfare. He told Ogden they had come close many times, but were not quite there with the antidote. Fearing that he might confiscate his parrot, he was careful not to mention that Plato was infected.

"So, you're sayin' you might have brought home the bug that got Margaret sick?"

"Yes, I believe I may have, but there is so much I still don't know."

"Mr. Harbinger, are you contagious? Can I get this thing just from bein' here?"

"No. I swabbed my nasal passages and what I found under the scope showed no signs of the bacteria," Harbinger explained. "I caught a bad case of parrot fever when I was younger and I'm immune."

Deep in thought, Ogden stared at his hands. "Well, can you call in your team and have your co-workers help you get this resolved? We need backup ASAP."

Harold felt glum at the overwhelming proposition, but nodded in consent. "I'll do my best."

Chapter 7 – Zombie Flock

True C. psittaci is a disease that hits birds with hookbills known as psittacines, (pronounced "sit-a-seen") such as parrots, parakeets and macaws. But, when other birds contract the diseases it is called ornithosis. The first widespread outbreak of this disease in the United States was in 1929 and it was so severe it lead to more restrictions on the importation of pet parrots as well as the establishment of the National Institute of Health.

The disease can effectively be treated with powerful antibiotics, but people with compromised immune systems have been known to die as a result. Humans contract the disease from infected droppings, nasal secretions or being near an infected bird or even eating eggs that were produced by birds carrying the bacteria.

To date Harold and his team had found that they could cure a sick bird, but had not even come close to creating a vaccine to prevent them from contracting it to begin with. It was a frustration they faced day after day and were actually at the point of asking their supervisor if they could change projects in order to more effectively use their talents as bird experts. But, Harold had been staying late some nights working on his own vaccine and those samples were his only hope.

After Ogden left, Harold asked himself if he should assemble his team or if there was a better way to head off this unavoidable and ungodly epidemic that was about to ravish his town and adjoining areas. He knew the bizarre deaths and attacks were going to make the papers and news programs, but Ogden had promised to keep Harold's name out of it as long as possible. Also, to keep mass hysteria from taking over, the police were controlling what information was given to the press.

Harold decided to wait and call the key members of his team in the morning. He was out of words for today, but hoped that in the a.m. he could explain the situation as simply as possible and ask his coworkers to brainstorm together and create a vaccine to shut down this mess.

He put on his pajamas just as he always did, drank a hot cup of chamomile tea, sharing a few sips with Plato, read poetry and tried to keep breathing, living, and moving forward without Margaret. The words in his book were far too blurry this night as tears effortlessly and limitlessly flowed down his cheeks. It was right then in his favorite chair doing all the things he had once known as comforts that he realized he and the world would never be the same. Because of one bacteria gone rogue he had lost too much already and would likely lose it all, perhaps within days. His pajama top was practically sopping on his chest, but he didn't have the energy to change.

Plato, tired from the day's events and ready for his favorite part of the daily ritual, pulled Harold's pajama top forward, ducked his head inside then burrowed down into the warmest spot right under Harold's right arm. "Harold, I love you! Night, Night."

This usually produced a huge smile from Harold and Margaret as well as she watched from the chair beside him. But not this night; everything was in its place, rituals were in tack, but Harold was not. He used his left sleeve to swipe the snot from his upper lip then rose slowly to head for the bedroom. "Night night time, Plato," he said reaching in and pulling the bird up onto his hand.

Plato leaned forward. "How's about a kiss, baby," he uttered before planting three sweet pecks on Harold's lips. Harbinger gently put the bird in his cage and latched the door before burrowing under his own disheveled covers. Without Margaret here, there seemed no point in making the bed anymore.

--

Harold had always been an early riser and relished the mornings and all the rituals that came with them such as his cup of Earl Grey tea, the morning paper and sitting on the back deck watching the birds. This morning he rose before the sun and trudged towards the kitchen. It was still dark outside and Plato was still in his roost mode and sleeping peacefully. Harold shuffled towards the sink, leaned against the counter and peered out the window. He could just see a hint of light on the horizon and knew it was at least an hour before there would be enough light to go outside and watch the birds feeding at the feeders and splashing in the many bird baths.

He turned on the stove to heat the kettle and pulled one of his favorite cups from the cupboard, handling it gingerly. Margaret's mother had given them the set of cups and saucers as a wedding gift. Each mug was delicately painted with images of different types of

British birds, one per cup. They captured the English charm with earth tones and realistic images. His favorite in the batch was the one with a European Robin because the bird was colorful, petite and was so delicate it looked like a cartoon version of an American Robin. *Oh, what I wouldn't give to hold one in my hands for just one minute*, thought Harold.

After the water boiled, he allowed the tea to steep then went back to the kitchen sink to observe the sunrise. He blew on his brew and prepared to take the first sips, but then he noticed two of the largest turkey vultures he had ever seen roosting in his biggest tree in the backyard. Their heads were tucked under their wings and they seemed deep in slumber. "Hmmm, never had buzzards in the back before," Harold thought out loud. He blew on his tea again and took a reassuring sip. There he stood for countless minutes watching the sun rise slowly and enjoying each taste. It was not until he reached forward to set the cup in the sink that he saw movement in the big tree. There was enough light now for him to realize they were not turkey vultures, but humans nestled in his branches. He didn't realize he had dropped the cup until he heard it shatter in the porcelain sink.

He immediately took the binoculars from the hook beside the sink; he and Margaret kept them there to get a better view of birds that visited their feeders. He was not prepared for what he saw, not in the least. His next door neighbors, the Johansens, were perched together snuggled in close right on a thick lower branch. They were well into their eighties, Mrs. Johansen had to use a walker to get around, and Harold was baffled by how they had made it up into the tree to begin with. The limb was sturdy, but he was shocked it had held the weight of both of them for the night.

Harold slid on his slippers and went outdoors, flashlight in hand, as stealthily as possible. Ten feet from the tree he shone the light directly at the Johansens. Both slowly raised their heads and looked in his direction, their normally sparkly eyes looking dingy and grey. Harbinger took off running towards the house, his heart keeping pace with his racing feet, he tripped over a sprinkler and went head first into a bush beside the porch. He scrambled up, darted inside the house, slamming then locking the door. "Oh what a beautiful moooooorninnngg, oh what a beautiful daayyy," sang Plato from the bedroom.

Harold ducked low then crawled into the bedroom so the Johansens could not see him through the windows. Safe inside his room he found his pants that contained his cell phone as well as the business card of Bill Stetson, the highway patrol man who had promised to help. He had seen Margaret at her worst, and he had been the one to end her misery. Without a second thought he dialed Stetson's number. Plato continued his morning serenade despite the hushing Harold was dishing out. After several rings Stetson answered sounding very much like he had been awoken from sleep.

"Officer Stetson?" Harold managed to ask between gulps of air as he breathed and tried to calm his frantic pulse.

"Yes, who's this?"

Harold felt his body begin to relax. He cleared his throat. "This is Harold Harbinger and this might sound crazy, but . . . "

Stetson cut him off quickly and asked him first to call him Bill and secondly told him to stay calm, that whatever it was he could be there in a half hour to help. Stetson saw the cemetery scene all over again and the anguish he felt for being the one to end Margaret Harbinger's life. As Harold described the elderly couple in the backyard tree and how birdlike they appeared Stetson felt his own heart begin to gallop. *God help us all – this is the beginning of the end,* he thought to himself.

"Harold, I need you to keep all the doors locked and stay away from the windows," he said with more calm than he thought he possessed. "Did you happen to call the police?"

"Police, no, I didn't think of that," Harold smoothed back his hair. "Should I get them over here too?"

"I'm afraid if we have the police involved as well, your sweet, old neighbors might not make it through this alive."

Harold nodded in agreement then thought how silly the gesture was considering Stetson could not see him. "Okay, I'll sit tight until you get here." He hung up without a goodbye.

He had just finished his call with Stetson when Harold heard a scraping sound coming from the back deck. He crawled to the blinds in his bedroom and lifted part of one slat in order to get a view of the deck. Now that he was closer to Plato, the bird began to sing more loudly. "Oh what a beautiful morning, Oh what a beautiful day."

From his obscured view through the blinds, Harbinger saw the Johansens turn towards the singing. Mr. Johansen, who had been in better shape before the bacteria claimed him, slowly shuffled towards the bedroom window, while his wife, who had needed a walker to get around, crawled in his direction. She was missing both shoes and her glasses hung precariously from her left ear. Foot by foot they slowly made their way until they were touching the glass of his bedroom window. Harold quickly dropped the part of the blind he had been holding and sat back. Mr. Johansen scraped his fingernails down the glass as if he knew Harold was just inches away. They sound of the scraping went on for minutes before it was replaced by a squeaking sound that Harold could not comprehend. He inched forward and risked another look. Apparently Mr. Johansen had lost his dentures sometime after the bacteria converted him, because he was gumming the glass, trying to chew through to get to his breakfast – Harold.

The bedroom was suddenly very still and silent. Harold looked at Plato and saw that the bird was sensing the fear, aggression and anxiety. Plato's eyes dilated, he fluffed the feathers on his neck and made growling sounds Harold had never heard. The bird tilted his head sideways and listened intently to the ceaseless squeaking at the window. Those sounds were joined by what must have been Mrs. Johansen pounding on the window beside her husband. Plato threw himself at the bars to get closer to the noise and began making shrill threatening sounds.

Harold watched in amazement; he had always known Plato was intelligent, but without even being able to see outside, Plato knew there were two intruders intent on hurting Harold. Plato's shrieks seemed to agitate the couple even more. It was as if they were members of the same flock and communicating with each other and working out the pecking order. Scientist that he was, he allowed his brain to take in the information and analyze it. *Was it possible that Plato thought of the Johansens as birds? Could he be calling out as a way of marking his territory? Or was he simply an animal reacting by instinct to a foreign sound?*

He could have thought of the logical choice that Plato was simply an animal, but there was something crazed about his bird, as if something had switched on his territorial switch and he was set on protecting what was his. He also seemed determined to demonstrate that he was the leader of the flock. To test his theory, Harbinger lifted the latch to Plato's cage. Plato flew straight to the side window and began throwing himself against the blinds and squawking. Within seconds the squeaking and scratching from the outside ceased and Plato sat listening, his feathers still fluffed to full height around his neck and his eyes dilating, his irises looking brighter yellow than ever.

Seconds went by and the silence remained. Calmed by the quiet, Plato moved to Harold's shoulder, Harbinger lifted one lower blind slightly, just enough to get a view of the porch. The Johansens had their backs turned and were trudging their way towards the back lawn, their heads bobbing forward as they went just like many species of birds did as they walked. It was a pitiful sight to behold. They had been the kind of neighbors who delivered cookies during the holidays and brought in the paper when the Harbingers were out of town. Who or what exactly they were now he could not fathom; they seemed more like birds than humans.

Harold realized that if he didn't act quickly the Johansens would crawl out of his yard and make their way to the next house. It was still a good twenty minutes before Stetson would arrive and help; it was up to Harbinger to stop them. He raised the blind so that he could have full view of them as they proceeded to the next house. The worst part for him was knowing he was the likely cause of their current condition. Somehow he had brought the bacteria home with him and it was on the move and taking over. The birds didn't seem harmed by the bacteria, but he knew without doing the math, that countless humans were going to die because of his carelessness.

Harold ran options through his mind. *How do I help? I don't have a gun, I can't physically stop them without getting hurt, or worse*. He looked at Plato as though his pet could problem solve. Plato shook himself, dust from his feathers bursting into the air and dancing in the morning sunlight that came through the window. As his dust settled so did his nerves and Plato began grooming himself. Harold put him back in his cage and scooped a cupful of seed into his dish.

Plato made a purring sound and began cracking the seed as if the Johansens had never been there. "Thank you, Harold," Plato cooed. "Love you, Harold," he croaked before resuming breakfast.

Harbinger looked out the window and leaned to the side far enough to see the Johansens advancing into the Miller's backyard. He hadn't had much of a social life over the years, but he spent enough time in the yard to know his neighbors well. He reached for his cell and scanned through contacts. He pushed the button for the Millers and hoped they would be quick to pick up. He had no idea if they were home and their hedge was so thick that once the Johansens entered the Miller's backyard, he would have no view of them. The phone rang until Harold heard the voice message. He paused momentarily, knowing he had to choose his words carefully. "Hello, this is Harold. This is an emergency, please call me as soon as you can and whatever you do, don't go outside. Lock all your doors." Harold felt as pathetic and useless as the message he had left. If they didn't hear it in time it wouldn't matter. Harsher thoughts slammed him *What if the Millers have already caught it? What if they are like the Johansens or dead?*

Harold felt sweat dripping down his sides and soaking his armpits. He realized there was one thing the Johansens and Millers had in common was bird feeders. In fact, several families along their street had feeders and kept them stocked with seed. He and Margaret had started the bird addiction on their lane by giving out seed dispensers as gifts at Christmas, as well as specialty blends that were already shelled and limited the mess beneath the feeders. Margaret had thought of it as a way to share the love of birding and to help supplement the diets of the wild birds.

It was at least fifteen minutes before Stetson would arrive and he knew he had to do something or the Millers could get their eyes scraped out by the Johansens. Hoping the front of the house was clear, he peered through the windows then quickly unlocked the door and slipped into the daylight and front yard. The Johansens were nowhere in sight so he ran quickly to the front door of the Millers and rang the bell. He listened and waited – nothing. He rang the bell again and got the same result. He stood still and listened for any sounds coming from the backyard. He heard chattering from sparrows, likely in the trees surrounding the Miller's feeders and the dog down the street was barking as usual. He thought he heard a sound of something being dragged across the lawn, but assumed it was his imagination.

He swiped the sweat from his forehead and walked as quietly as possible across the front porch and peeked around the corner to the side yard. What he saw stunned him; Mr. Johansen had the hand of Mrs. Johansen and was dragging her behind him. Her glasses were nowhere to be seen and Mr. Johansen seemed determined to keep her with him, occasionally looking back at her and making grunting sounds. She looked up at him, drooling and making guttural sounds. At that moment Harold had no fear because he knew he could easily outrun them. What fascinated him was that fact that they were sticking together. Many species of birds choose a mate and stick together for life and it appeared the Johansens were no exception. He was touched by the sadness and sweetness of their predicament until Mr. Johansen looked up and saw Harold watching them. The expression that came over his face was one of a hunter that had spied its prey. He dropped his wife's arm and started a faster shuffle straight at Harbinger.

Harold sprinted to his house, made it inside, slammed the door and locked both locks. His heart was rapping against his ribs just like the woodpecker he had seen drilling a hole in their cottonwood last week. The thunk, thunk of his heart sounded a lot like the pounding the tree trunk had received. He leaned against the door and braced himself for the worst. He heard the squeak of the last front step as Mr. Johansen stepped up, a dragging sound and then moaning and garbled words as Mr. Johansen, liberated from his dentures, mumbled threatening sounds.

A deep and resonating voice sounded from the front of his house. "Put your hands up and get down on your knees," shouted Stetson.

Johansen was not the least bit distracted by the presence of Bill Stetson and continued clawing at the front door. Johansen was set on his prey. Harold moved to the windows and drew back the curtain to see what was happening outside. He could clearly see Stetson and the pistol he brandished in front of him. "Sir, I repeat, put your hands up and get down on your knees." It was not until that moment that Stetson noticed Mrs. Johansen crawling towards him commando style using her elbows to pull her ancient body.

Stetson didn't waste a second and jogged to his car, got inside and locked the doors before grabbing his cell and calling for help. The police department picked up after several minutes. "911, is this an emergency? If it is not please call later we are having a huge volume of calls," said the harried woman.

"This is Bill Stetson, highway patrolman and I have an emergency and need police backup immediately." As Stetson spoke, Mrs. Johansen grabbed the passenger handle and pulled herself up until she was looking into his car. Stetson was more resentful than ever at that moment for being suspended as his patrol car was much sturdier than the compact car he drove. From the front porch, Mr. Johansen responded to his wife's guttural calls for help and limped in her direction. With both attackers focused on him he felt queasy and saw how shaky his hands had become. He had surrendered his pistol to his superiors when he was suspended, but he had his trusty Beretta nine millimeter that he had owned for years. More than his hands were shaking now as the Johansens began to pound the windows and rock the car. They seemed much stronger than they should have been considering their obvious advanced age.

His mind could clearly see Margaret Harbinger and how she was tearing apart the EMTs at the cemetery. He knew even though these people were old, they could still inflict some serious damage. Looking at them was too much. *This is like a scene from a bad zombie movie*, he thought to himself. Seeing their grey eyes and drooling mouths disgusted him and he turned his focus to his connection with the police department. "I'm under attack by two civilians and I'm in my car in desperate need of backup," Bill practically shouted. "When can a squad car get here?" Before they could answer Mr. Johansen climbed onto the hood of the car and turned to pull his wife up with him. She slid easily across the hood and landed with her face pressed against the glass, her drool smearing the window. Stetson dropped the phone and knew he was disconnected. When he looked up he saw Mrs. Johansen staring Stetson straight in the eyes, her own pupils dilating and retracting. She clawed at the glass and inched towards the driver's side of the car. Stetson sat back as far as he could in his seat, but it was no use because each detail of their faces was still perfectly clear. His nose covered with tiny red veins that looked very much like blood worms and his pock-marked cheeks were bad enough, but beside him was his wife and her lined and withered face, they seemed monstrous as they pressed closer to the glass. Mr. Johansen opened his mouth and began to gum and lick the window. His tongue was coated with a white substance that reminded Stetson of spoiled milk and he thought he would vomit. Mr. Johansen began to claw at the window, clearly not understanding the futility of his actions. Soon their two faces were side by side gnawing at the thick glass with their gums; the squeaking sounds were maddening. *Sounds like a batch of mice being tortured*, thought Stetson. Mrs. Johansen pulled herself up and onto the top of the car just far enough that Stetson could see her soiled depends and baggy, torn pantyhose.

Bill heard a loud bashing sound; had it been in a comic book would have been spelled something like

"Thwank." He turned to his left and saw Harold Harbinger effectively smashing each of the attackers in the head with a heavy garden shovel.

--

As they dragged the bodies into the backyard towards the tool shed both men agreed that having the police involved at this moment would be a disaster for both of them. Stetson was already suspended, and Harbinger would likely be arrested. They spoke as they moved the bodies.

"I think I know what's going on and how this sickness began," Harold said as he paused to wipe sweat from his brow and to make sure no neighbors were watching.

"What? What's happening and how do you know about it?" asked Stetson as they stacked the bodies in the shed and secured it with a cheap combination lock Harold had picked up years before.

"How about we go inside, wash our hands and I'll tell you about it."

Safe inside the house all doors double locked, Harold relaxed, but had the presence of mind to keep Stetson away from the kitchen and Plato's droppings. They settled in the formal parlor, a place where Plato rarely visited.

While they sat and reclaimed their calm, Harold told what he knew of the bacteria, his research to find a cure, the history of psittacosis and how he felt personally responsible for somehow bringing home a mutated bacteria to Margaret.

"What makes you think you had anything to do with Margaret getting it?" Stetson asked.

"When I saw her at the morgue I took swabs and a collection tube," he explained. "What I found in her sinuses was a mutated version of the bacteria we've been working with." He continued his story with details about how he had contracted psittacosis years before and that was why he was immune to the bacteria, about Plato and several wild birds also hosting the mutated germ. "They don't seem to have any symptoms, but are clearly carriers. My guess is that, just like with psittacosis, breathing in spores from the droppings is the way humans are contracting the disease."

Stetson rubbed his temples and stared at the table. "You got any aspirin? I have a hell of a headache."

Harbinger brought him the pain killer and a cup of coffee. "I have a plan," blurted Harold.

"A plan? Am I involved in this in any way?" Stetson asked before popping all three pills into his mouth and washing it down with coffee.

"Well, not at first. I need to get into the lab and bring home our most recent antidote as well as a batch I've been working on by myself and see if it can make a difference, first with Plato. If it can kill the bacteria in his body, perhaps we have a way to wipe it out in all the wild birds as well before the entire community catches it." Harold ruffled his hair, "On second thought, I would like to inject you to see if we can prevent you from catching it."

Stetson nodded his approval then stared at the dregs in his cup and swished around the last drops of brew. "They even know what's happened to your wife?"

"Who?" asked Harold as he cleaned his glasses, put them back on then turned to look out the window.

"Your coworkers, your friends at work."

"Oh, I really have no idea," Harold mumbled. "I haven't called in, I guess word got to them somehow." *Friends*? Harold thought to himself. His only true friends had been Margaret and Plato. They sat in an awkward silence until Stetson sat forward and put his cup on the coffee table.

"Tell you what, buddy. You make some calls to the office, get together a plan for this antidote of yours then let me know what the next step is," he said with forced cheerfulness. The realization that Harold was a typical scientist without a social network and team of friends occurred to him and the sadness of it, especially at this tragic moment in Harold's life, made him feel exhausted. "I'm awful tired. I'll head home and get in a nap if I can, call me if you need me, and whatever you do, don't take the lock off that shed."

They stood by the front door both unsure what to say or do until Stetson decided a good manly pat on the back was the only appropriate show of support either could handle at that moment. He gave him three sturdy, manly pats the kind the guys in his unit said spoke volumes with each pat - *I'm Not Gay*. It was one of their many jokes, but Stetson didn't feel much like joking today. Before walking out he turned back for one last look at Harold; the sadness that was layers deep shone clearly in his eyes.

Chapter 8 – Antidote

Harold knew it would raise suspicion if he ventured into the lab before closing hours; his coworkers would wonder how he could be back so soon after his wife's demise. He waited until six before he headed to the Prius. After Stetson left that day and he had time to sit down and write a plan (he always thought more clearly if he could see it in writing), he spent time with Plato watching the bird intently, hoping somehow he would help Harold find the way or offer an answer to the enormous problem that loomed before them. But, Plato was Plato and demanded his favorite food, ran through his routine of favorite sayings and managed to convince Harold to wrestle with him. Even with that focused activity Harold's mind returned to Margaret over and over again. *Did I tell her enough that I loved her? Did she know how beautiful she looked in the morning light? Did I take time to show her she was the most incredible woman in the world?* Perhaps he would find peace within himself with time and know he had been good to her and that she knew how he adored her, perhaps.

Inside the car he turned on classical music, louder than usual, to soothe his nerves and keep his thoughts focused on his mission and off of Margaret. It customarily took less than twenty minutes to get to work, but Harold was shocked by the volume of police cruisers and even the stumbling humans who were obviously infected and wondered if he could still call them human; in his line of thinking they were somewhere between bird and man. Both humans and the others were jamming the streets of his neighborhood and making it very difficult to drive forward.

The police were trying to corral the staggering wanderers, but they were having a rough go of it as the infected were lunging towards their eyes and the police were using their tazers with a vengeance. The fire fighters had a more efficient means of controlling a mob and accessed the fire hydrants and began blasting the stumblers and forcing them into a massive group. Highway patrolmen began appearing at the scene as well as National Guard officers. All troops together ensured the crazed, squawking stumblers remained in a tight group where they could then be urged into police vans.

Harold pulled over to watch and realized the reports he had heard were correct; the people infected with the bacteria moved like birds in various ways. Some walked with their heads bobbing in front of them just like pigeons. Others flapped their arms out then rolled their hands into tight hook-like shapes and tried digging into eyes. The gouging out of eyes by birds had always perplexed Harold. It seemed to be a higher form of thinking that occurred in the aves as they instinctively knew to destroy the eyesight of other birds, usually smaller than themselves. He had witnessed many an attack in the field and it was usually a larger bird holding down a song bird and pecking straight into the eyes until all that remained were two bloody sockets. As a researcher he was not allowed to interfere, but he and Margaret both had to restrain themselves and not bolt in the direction of the attack and pull off the larger bird and protect the smaller one. It was one barbaric trait of the creatures that hurt him to the core. It was hard for him to fathom how such spiritual species could inflict such brutal and inevitably lethal force on birds much smaller than themselves. The tinier ones, once blinded, often died within minutes usually by shock or perhaps the result of countless blows to the interior skull.

Harold noticed a stumbler heading in his direction, put his car in reverse, and headed in the opposite direction that would take him the longer, but safer way to work. He gave one last look behind him and felt the pangs of guilt because he, Harold Harbinger, had set all this in motion.

When he finally reached Avetech, the research building that felt like home, there were very few cars in the lot. He saw Michael O'Brian walking to his car and ducked his head, trying not to be noticed. But, O'Brian waved and came towards his car. Harold rolled down the window.

O'Brian set down his briefcase and leaned on the window frame, his head slightly poking into the car. "Harold, I don't know what to say, man," he reached forward to hug Harold and changed his mind. "I guess I just want to say sorry about Margaret, she was an incredible woman." He twirled his keys on his finger and looked towards the building.

"Thank you. She was," Harold said before straightening the papers on the passenger seat.

"So, is there anything I or we can do to help?"

Harold stared at him, there were no needs, no explanations, no hopes. In the end he dropped his head and looked at the papers he had shifted to his lap.

After a long and extremely awkward pause, O'Brien cleared his throat. "So, the Center for Disease Control reps were here today and believe our lab and our research on the vaccine may have something to do with these crazy people and the attacks."

Harold stared straight ahead. "Hmmm."

"What do you think? They were asking all kinds of questions, some pretty crazy ones like why aren't the people who are attacked turning crazy too," O'Brien said as he leaned in closer. "I think they've all been watching too many zombie movies or something."

Harold adjusted the papers then smoothed the material of his pants and sat quietly staring at the steering wheel. Before O'Brien's comments he hadn't even thought of what had become of the many who had been attacked. He supposed it was a blessing to them and the general population that if you were bitten or scratched by someone who had been taken over by the bacteria that you did not acquire the illness. But what did he care? Margaret was gone.

O'Brien patted the car. "Well, I, um, better get going," he mumbled. "My wife has dinner ready." Instantly wishing he could gulp back his words, who was he to mention a spouse to Harold at a time like this?

Remembering why he had come, Harold forced himself to perform social niceties so that he would not appear suspicious. "See you later," he said before pushing the button to roll up the window. He gathered his belongings and left his car making sure to lock it before he walked away. And, as he always did, he turned back to click the lock button with his key one more time. By the time he was strolling towards the entrance, O'Brien was long gone.

The day felt layered with awkward moments, particularly when he passed through security and saw the shock on the faces of the two security men. Both looked at each other and were clueless as to how to greet Harold because he was the very last person they expected to see coming through the front door.

Harold nodded at them, ran his badge through the scanner and walked towards his office like he did any other weekday. Although he had made it through without a word spoken among them, he sensed their curiosity and pity. He hated the pity and more than that the reason behind it. He unlocked his office, entered and shut the door behind him. His world felt so tilted and wrong he expected his office to be disheveled or destroyed, but there it was tidy and in perfect order just as it had been days ago when he last worked.

He settled the papers on his desk then opened his briefcase. Inside he had several tubes, droppers, and syringes safely tucked into foam padding. He put on his lab coat and slipped all the supplies from the briefcase into his pockets. He knew the security guards had monitors to see what went on in the labs, but he was the senior researcher, the director in fact, and was allowed access and they paid little attention to what he did as he spent such long hours alone working on the vaccine and bacteria.

He strolled down the hallway acting as casual as possible and entered the restricted area of the building with the use of his security card. The research area was divided into two parts. The first zone contained equipment and compounds that the researchers used in their efforts to create a vaccine to prevent psittacosis. Customary laboratory caution was practiced there as they worked with a variety of substances, but the researchers felt safe because the actual lethal bacteria was not with them. The second area was considered hazardous because it contained vials of live bacteria and any person entering had to wear a biohazard suit to avoid contamination and infection. Computer monitors at the security station recorded all activity that occurred in zone two and daily reports were given to Harold for his inspection. However, because he was the senior researcher he could suit up, enter the area and work without being questioned as long as he did it when his coworkers had gone home, similar to this evening. His images and the time he spent in the lab would be in the daily report on his desk the next day, but it didn't matter.

Harold went to his locker, reached inside and put the vials and supplies within the exterior pockets of the biohazard suit. He then slid off his lab coat and stepped into the safety of the thick, white bio suit. Even though he knew there was not a camera in the dressing room, he couldn't help but turn around to make sure he wasn't being watched. He switched on the oxygen and proceeded into the danger zone.

A bio contaminant can be classified by the danger it poses to the surrounding environment. In 2006 four different biological safety levels ("BSL") were established by the American Biological Safety Association or better known as the "ABSA." These levels range from BSL1 through BLS4 – the higher the number, the more hazardous the biological substances are to the environment. Avetech, or what Harold thought of as his lab, was a BSL3, which meant it was up to him to determine whether the researchers had to wear full bio suits or just protective hoods and gloves. He chose the former. However, he did not require the decontamination showers after leaving the lab, nor the ultraviolet light room. There was an airlock that was electronically controlled and only opened for employees with higher level pass cards. All four members of his research team had those access cards.

With ease Harold scanned his card, the airlock opened and he stepped into the lab. He went straight to the common area where all four of his coworkers tested and retested vaccines for Chlamydia psittaci. He scanned the area and then looked straight ahead to his favorite part of the building, the room that contained the conures and other small parrots. He passed through another airlock and went to visit the birds he had come to cherish. Each squawked in recognition and jumped forward and clung to the bars hoping Harold would offer the regular treats. He walked to the end of the row of cages, opened the cupboard and brought out the bag of peanuts then he reached into the small refrigerator below and drew out several small oranges. He sliced the fruit and listened to the birds whistle and chatter in happy anticipation. He filled a dish with the orange slices and another with the peanuts and stopped at each cage.

With a hand covered in a latex glove he first scratched each head and neck and then tucked the treats in their food dishes. Within minutes all birds were happily crunching their treats, occasionally looking up at him with sparkly eyes. He stood back, folded his arms and watched them. He knew he was on an urgent errand, but this group of birds brought such instant and complete happiness into his life he could not pull himself away. As he sighed and watched them a thought occurred to him. *What if they too have the same bacteria in their systems as Plato?*

If they had the mutated bacteria they could be part of the epidemic. His logical mind told him to test all their stools for the presence of the bacteria, but his more compassionate thinking zone told him it was better not to know. If it was discovered these birds too had the lethal bacteria and were carriers he knew his superiors would order him to destroy the birds and the thought was too painful for him to fathom at that moment in his life. He turned quickly and left the room, making sure not to look back.

Back inside the lab he went straight to the climate-controlled cabinet that was his alone. It was where he kept his specimens for the antidote and his trial vaccines. He opened it up, drew out the trays of tubes and began the transfer of his serum into the tubes in his pocket. He returned the tray and locked his cupboard. Just in case any of his subordinates had been having luck with their antidote he stopped at the general cupboard and withdrew a vial. Mission accomplished, he leaned forward and rested his wrists on the counter. His weariness was deep and he leaned forward and placed his head on his crossed arms. From that view he noticed a small tear near the right wrist in his biohazard suit. He stared at it in disbelief. He leaned forward and could hear a small hissing sound as the air escaped.

Moving quickly, Harold grabbed a swab and rubbed around the area with the tear then smeared the findings on glass slides before putting them under the microscope. What he found was no surprise, but still it felt like a huge kick in the gut as he watched the mutated bacteria move about under the scope. His thinking had slipped in the past few days, he knew that, but it appeared the bacteria were swimming happily without a care in the world.

He sat down to think through the situation more clearly. If there was a hole in his suit and the very bacteria that were on it were the same type that killed Margaret he knew the source of her contracting the disease. The bacteria must have somehow gotten on his skin through the hole and he, assuming all was well, put his biohazard suit away, dressed in his street clothes and headed home unaware that he had dangerous passengers riding along with him as he traveled home to Margaret and Plato.

Think! Think, Harold, he told himself as he sat. His mind ticked through all the possibilities and the only logical conclusion was that some time recently he had entered the bird area, scratched enough heads and played with the research birds to pick up the bacteria from their nasal secretions. That bacteria had managed to make its way into the hole in his suit as it sought a warm, moist place to thrive. "That is it," he said aloud. "It can't live inside my body because I am immune, but it could have survived for hours, even days, plenty of time for me to take it home to my family." His face felt numb and the room seemed to swim in front of him. "*So this is what it feels like to pass out*," he thought. He had the presence of mind to bend forward and put his head between his knees. He took slow even breaths and noticed his heart had slowed its powerful rate as well. The tingling sensation in his face began to disappear and within a few minutes he was able to sit up and focus his thoughts on what to do next.

The traumatic reality that if he was a carrier of the lethal bacteria, it was likely his coworkers were as well as they handled the birds and had suffered parrot fever with him years ago. Together they were a toxic, disease spreading, immune group of humans. Their love of birds and their dedication to finding a cure for parrot fever was quite likely the reason countless humans were dying as he sat safely inside his lab. But, if that were true, wouldn't their family members start dropping as well? He didn't know how to move forward, if he should call them all in and test them or let it go because it didn't matter anymore, nothing did really. *But what about the tear in my suit*? He thought. He alone, as far as he knew, had a tear in his suit and he might be the only member of the team who dragged the bacteria home.

He patted his pockets and felt the vials were still safely tucked into the pockets of the suit. He eased himself up, walked to the drawers and removed several capped syringes and headed out of the lab. After he had disrobed and put the vials into his white lab coat he headed to his office.

A security officer approached him in the hall at a brisk pace, the clicking of his heels on the linoleum had never sounded so irritating. Harold felt his face turning hot.

"Everything okay, Mr. Harbinger?" The officer said as he tilted his head slightly to the side and took a deep look into Harold's eyes.

Harold started walking past him. "Of course," he said with a dismissive tone as he tried to keep his knees from shaking. "Heading home."

--

As Harold pulled onto his street he saw a police cruiser parked in front of his home. There was no point in trying to evade them; the inevitable awaited in a black squad car. As Harold turned into his driveway the officers opened their car doors and approached. Harbinger acted as nonchalant as possible. "Evening officers," he said as he turned to lock his car one more time, then fished through the ring of keys to find the one that matched the front door lock.

"Mr. Harbinger, we have some questions, sir," said the officer who appeared to be most senior between them. "Do you mind if we come in?"

Harold clutched the briefcase closer to him. "Come on in," he mumbled. But, before going to the front door he turned and clicked the lock button one more time because obsessive, compulsive behaviors were hard to turn off even in times of distress.

Inside the parlor both officers stood awkwardly and looked around the room. "Margaret, I am Home!" resonated from the bedroom. Both heads whipped in unison in the direction Plato's call.

Harold walked into the kitchen and put his briefcase on the counter before turning to look at the officers. "That's my parrot, Plato, he is quite the mimic."

The officers relaxed at his explanation and looked back and forth at each other. "Sir, I'm Officer Gomez, and as you are probably aware, there have been several attacks on your street alone during the past two days," the senior officer explained. His soft brown eyes shone with sincerity and seemed to plead with Harold for help. His words were unnecessary; Harold understood how desperate they were if they were willing to approach a grieving man who had already been questioned.

Harold straightened a doily on the armchair. "Would you like to sit while we talk?"

"Sir, that is not necessary," said the second, much younger officer as he pulled out his notebook and prepared to take notes.

Harold sat in the armchair, looking very much like the king of the castle. "Begin."

The officers looked at each other, then around the room. "Sir, excuse me for not introducing myself earlier, I'm Officer Taylor," he said with a tone of respect. "We understand you're a bird expert and that you might know what's happening to these people who are, if you will excuse the expression, crazy as bird shit and on a killing spree," said the younger officer as he looked at his partner for approval.

Harold thought of his briefcase and the vials within and took his time in answering. "I am aware that my wife became very ill and died in our car on the way to the hospital, I'm told she somehow resurrected in the ambulance and killed two paramedics," he said with a shaky voice. "It was also brought to my attention that the same woman I had been with and loved for over twenty years allegedly tried to kill a man at the cemetery and that she was shot in the head." Harold straightened his pants and stared down the officers.

Gomez put his hand up in a type of peace gesture. "Forgive us, Mr. Harbinger, we know you've been through so much, but you have to understand, our most recent count of dead bodies, including those infected with the sickness, is over fifty now, basically an epidemic."

Harold cleared his throat and clutched the arms of the chair. "And, what exactly do you think I can do to help you?"

"Details sir, we need details about what is causing the sickness," Gomez answered.

Harold was eager to get to his vaccine and try it on Plato, or perhaps Bill Stetson first, but he had to play nice and help the officers as much as possible without giving away too much information. "As I explained to Mr. Ogden when he visited me, I have some ideas as to how the sickness began, but as to why it is spreading and the aggressive behavior that accompanies it, I have no clue."

Gomez sat on the couch closest to Harbinger and leaned forward. "How, exactly, is the virus spreading? And why is it that people who are bitten are not acquiring the sickness as well?"

"It is not a virus, it is a bacteria," Harbinger corrected him. "It is related to the bacteria we work with at the lab, but appears to be a mutated form of it. It's most likely that I somehow brought home the germ and transferred it to my wife." Harold was surprised that he felt his throat tighten making it difficult to spit out the next words. "I, um, guess you could say I killed my wife by infecting her." As much as he tried to prevent it, tears began to trickle down his cheeks.

Gomez reached out to pat Harbinger's knee, but thought better of it and retracted his hand. "Is there a cure? Are you aware of any vaccine we can use to cure these people once they are infected?"

Harold wiped his eyes on his sleeve. "At our lab we were able to cure birds infected with psittaci bacteria with antibiotics, but I have no idea if it will work on this mutated bacteria," Harold explained. "You can go to Avetech directly and request the antibiotics from anyone on my team, grab the vaccines we are working on while you are at it, but I don't know what else I can do for you." Harold wanted to end the conversation, but felt a twinge of bitterness. "I was informed the CDC visited my workplace today, perhaps they can help you," Harold dropped his head into his hands and ran his fingers through his thick, coarse hair. With a lowered head, and eyes clamped shut, he spoke slowly and angrily, "My wife is dead! I am exhausted and tired of all these questions!"

Both officers knew he was at his breaking point. Gomez spoke first, "We're so sorry for your loss and for the inconvenience," he said. "We will obtain everything we can from your lab tomorrow and the CDC and, hopefully, begin saving these people."

As they turned to leave Taylor couldn't resist one more question. "Mr. Harbinger, why are they acting like birds?"

Harold's eyes snapped open. He was beyond tired and so wrapped up in sorrow and bitterness, at that moment he didn't care if Plato walked onto their shoulders, sneezed into their open mouths and infected them. "Why don't you ask them yourself, I don't care."

As they left he shut the door harder than he intended.

Chapter 9 – Ten Birds With One Stone

Happy Times daycare was tiny, but the staff was dedicated to the children they cared for. The small building was painted bright blue with purple trim around the windows. The front yard was fenced and packed with play gear. The building itself was enough to make even adults smile.

Jen was the huggy, playful one who loved playing with the kids and watching them learn and acquire new skills. She had long, shiny blond hair and often wore it in braids just as the little girls did. Her work partner, Sophie, was caramel brown with thick black hair cut in a fashionable bob. She was proud of her Spanish heritage and always wore colorful clothing, fingernail polish and plenty of lipstick. As a team they were irresistible to small children. They daycare had opened a year earlier and they only took in eight kids at a time in order to give them maximum attention. Their current roster contained three boys and five girls ranging in age from three to five. Happy Times was a place of refuge and peace while their parents worked.

"Summer is the perfect time to go to the zoo," Jen chirped as she announced the daily field trip to the kids. "Get your backpacks kiddos, we're heading to the Los Angeles Zoo."

Shrieks of delight resounded throughout the daycare and its colorful walls.

Jen checked each pack to make sure there was a lunch, a bottle of water and sunscreen. "Check and double check!" she exclaimed. "It's off to the zoo we go."

Sophie had prepared the van by turning on the air conditioner and making sure all seats were clean and that seatbelts were in working order. "All cutie pies line up in a straight line, smallest in front," she said with a huge smile as the zoo was her favorite destination to take children. "Who's ready for fun?"

"We are!" shouted all the children in unison.

The drive to the zoo was brief, but the group managed to sing countless travel songs as they went. Jen started to think if she heard "Wheels on the Bus" one more time she might develop a headache. But her cheeriness won out and she kept smiling, humming and singing until they were parked and ready to line up at the front gates. As was their tradition, they headed up the stairs to the right and straight into the nursery. The children squealed in delight as they saw the baby sea otters in the play pens. A worker at the zoo was inside the nursery with the tiny, squirming babies, holding them one at a time, feeding each a bottle and treating them as if they were human babies. The little girls in particular pressed close to the glass watching each move and hearing every meow of the little orphans. It was more than a half hour before Jen and Sophie could persuade them to move on.

The temptation of the reptile house was what got all eight children moving out of the building and up the path towards the zone where the creepiest creatures at the zoo could be found lurking at a safe distance behind the glass. The docents in the building politely reminded the children not to tap on the glass and to speak in quiet tones in order to keep the reptiles and amphibians from becoming frightened. The little boys lead the way, showing the girls how it was done when it came to "real animals". Moving their way through the building the kids adored the tiny frogs and beamed as they spied the vibrant colors. The docent explained that the brilliant colors served as a warning to other wild animals that these little creatures were poisonous and shouldn't be eaten. After the frogs, they squatted low to get an eye level view of the python. After they had their fill of scaly creatures, they opened the exit doors and walked into the bursting sunshine. Up ahead on the path they noticed a woman holding a very large red bird.

"No running and hold hands so that you don't get separated," cautioned Sophie.

As they came to the end of the path, the older woman holding the bird explained that it was a scarlet macaw and that he had been hand-raised at the zoo and was very friendly. The bird's name was Hibiscus and each child could hold him and have his or her photo taken for a small donation to the zoo.

The children began jumping up and down. "Please, please can we hold the birdie?"

Jen looked skeptical "How much?" she asked the docent.

"Whatever you can afford," the docent replied before covering her mouth with the crook of her elbow in hopes of suppressing a loud cough.

Jen and Sophie looked at each other. Sophie put her hands on her knees. "Okay, line up, smallest to tallest."

One at a time the children allowed the huge bird to perch on their shoulders. Jen snapped pictures of each child and would email the photos to the parents before the day's end. She relished her job as the photographer of the group and knew the parents adored photographs. Most likely, all the kids happy faces would end up on Facebook before bedtime.

The docent turned to Jen. "How about you? He seems to be leaning towards you like he would like to be friends."

The kids cheered and encouraged Jen to share in the fun. She handed the camera to Sophie and let the parrot climb onto her shoulder. She wasn't expecting it to have such a pungent, overwhelming odor. "What is that smell?" she asked the docent.

"Most birds have a limited sense of smell, but all have their own unique odor," she explained. "In the bird world macaws have one of the strongest smells. I happen to like it."

Jen was about to hand Hibiscus to Sophie when the parrot leaned over and kissed Jen on the lips with its huge beak and snake-like black tongue darting out to touch her lower lip. Jen scrunched her eyes closed. The docent, sensing, Jen's discomfort, took the bird and offered it to Sophie, but because Sophie had on her usual bright lipstick and bright red fingernail polish the bird hesitated then stepped tentatively onto Sophie's shoulder. The docent explained that certain colors are warning colors to birds, particularly if they were in the red family.

Sophie seemed confused by this information. "That doesn't make any sense. He's red."

"I can't explain it; that is just the way they are. Many animals are afraid of red. Also, this is a parrot we are talking about and they are particular – either they like you or they don't," explained the docent, sounding out of patience.

The docent pulled her t-shirt forward and coughed loudly inside. "Sorry, I'm catching a cold and don't want my germs to get to the kids," she explained.

Sophie lost all enthusiasm in the bird and the kids were ready to move on. Before she could hand the macaw back to its keeper, Hibiscus sneezed loudly and wetly in Sophie's face. She grimaced and pulled an anti-bacterial wipe from her backpack and hastily cleaned her skin.

She had to pick up her pace to catch up with the kids ahead on the trail. *Disgusting! Bird buggers right on my face and in my eye. I've had enough of the zoo for one day*, she thought to herself.

Within an hour the entire group of ten was feeling lethargic and some were complaining of headaches. They barely touched their lunches and Jen and Sophie knew it was time to return to Happy Times.

--

At 5 p.m. on the dot parents began lining up in the cars in front of the daycare. Usually Jen and Sophie were punctual and were outside with the kids and helped each little tot get safely inside their cars and secured the seatbelts. As the line grew longer and the parents' patience grew shorter, it became apparent that all was not well or happy inside Happy Times.

Charles Henry was the first in line, and being a born Californian he honked his horn to get the attention of the daycare workers. He waited less than a minute before he honked again.

The woman behind him, Connie Smith, tapped on his window. "There's no need to be rude," she chided. "Handling children is tougher than you think." Connie walked away from his car straight towards the front door of the bright blue building. She had to maneuver through the obstacle course of toys and tricycles before she reached the steps. As she prepared to take the three steps up she realized how very quiet it was inside the building; as a mother she had known for years that quiet wasn't always a good thing. She hesitated before opening the door. She put her hand on the handle and thought better of it and rapped loudly. "Hello, any little ones ready to go home?"

Connie tilted her head towards the door and leaned in closer. What she heard confused her, it sounded like clucking sounds. *I must be losing my marbles*, she thought. Suddenly the thought of opening the door was so frightening she pulled out her cell and called the daycare. As the rings sounded throughout the building the clucking sounds intensified and on top of that she heard grumbling, garbled sounds that were childlike, but noises no human should be making. Panic crept up inside her and she felt her throat tighten. *Oh, God, no! Not a panic attack right now*, she thought as she rummaged through her purse for her valium.

Charles Henry stomped up the steps and planted himself beside her. "What ya waitin' for? Just open the door and go on in," he snarled. "This is going to get me stuck right in the middle of heavy traffic and I'll have to listen to whining all the way home."

Connie tried to warn him, but he pushed past her, opened the door wide and prepared to step inside. He thought he had seen a lot in his life, but the vision before him was something from a graphic novel. The two women were near the back of the room each on top of a desk with the children clustered behind them. The ladies had their arms held out wide, their heads held low and their stares were piercing. Their fingers were curled up in a claw-like fashion and the children stood behind them as if they were the only protection they had in the world. The women made garbled clucking sounds. *I have gone straight to crazy land - they sound like damn chickens*, Charles thought as he took a step back.

Remembering the stories of crazy locals acting like birds attacking and even killing people, he shut the door then he and Connie retreated together, walking backwards towards the line of cars while Connie dialed 911. Charles tripped on a toy and went down hard on his backside. Within minutes police cars and parents were swarming in front of the building.

All officers recited the quotes they had memorized in police academy. "Stay calm, help is on the way, everything is going to be just fine," they practically chanted in unison, but little that they said calmed the parents.

"Those are our children in there with those crazy women," one bold mother blurted out only to be corrected by Charles.

"Miss, it's not just the adults, the children have it to and they're acting like chicks trying to take cover under their mother hens," Charles explained. "I wouldn't believe it either, but I saw it for myself."

The leader of the brigade of police, Darren Ogden, spoke up. "The last thing we want to do is use force and have any of the children injured, or worse," he said with authority. "We're going to bring in a bird expert to help us control the people in the building without anyone getting hurt."

Ogden pulled an officer aside. "I don't care what it takes, get Harbinger over here right now to help us sort out this mess," he said before removing his sunglasses and leaning forward. "Make the call where parents can't hear you I don't want anything to happen to those kids or It'll be my job on the line."

As the officer prepared to make the call Bill Stetson drove up the street, parked and walked into the middle of the drama. "I heard on the radio and wondered if I could help."

Ogden stared at him, his lips set in a thin, hard line. "So, why would I need a highway patrolman who is currently suspended," he asked. "Want to enlighten me as to how you're so valuable?"

"Sir, to begin with, I'm friends with Mr. Harbinger and I might be able to persuade him to help," he said gently, hoping to ease the tension. "Also, I've dealt with people inflicted with this disease already."

Ogden put his shades back on and turned his back. "That's just the problem, we don't need you shootin' anyone else."

Stetson felt the old kick in the groin all over again and knew he was never going to live down shooting Margaret Harbinger. "Sir, that's exactly why I'm not a problem, I know what to expect, how they attack, how to protect myself and everyone else here."

Ogden stopped, he didn't turn to acknowledge Stetson, but looked for the younger officer. "What did Harbinger say? Is he coming?" he asked using the harshest voice he could muster – no highway patrolman was going to outdo him today.

"Sir, he answered, but he said he's much too busy to come to the scene," the young officer said before gulping.

Ogden scowled. "He's just a few miles from here, what could be so important that he can't make the trip to help these kids?"

The parents were turning into a mob. "We want our kids outta there and right now!"

Stetson walked towards Ogden. "Sir, let me try, he'll listen to me."

Ogden barked at him. "Just make your damn call and get him over here!"

Stetson did as he was ordered, but when Harbinger answered he seemed just as reluctant. "Listen, buddy, I came to you when you called me," he reminded him. "There's a bunch a scared moms and dads here and you may be the only person who can help us get these kids out without any injuries."

The silence on the other end of the phone lasted much longer than Stetson anticipated. "Harold, you there?"

"I'm thinking," Harold answered, his words coated with frustration. All he wanted was to try his vaccine and try to clean the bacteria out of Plato's system. But, the police and their nonstop drama kept him from what he really wanted. Harold let out a long breath. "Okay, first thing they should do is call in animal control with three big vans," Harold said. "Make sure all the animal control workers have the long poles with loops on the end, the type they use on aggressive dogs. I'll be there as soon as possible."

Before leaving he prepared an injection of doxycycline for Plato. He would have put powder in the bird's water, but unfortunately he was a picky eater and drinker thanks to the way he and Margaret had spoiled him over the years. He filled a hypodermic, grabbed a bath towel, wrangled Plato into the towel so that he could not see and would stay calm and then gave him an injection in the leg. He hoped when he returned home Plato's droppings would have fewer of the live bacteria in them.

The drive should have been short, but cars moved slowly, clogging the flow of traffic. Up ahead he could see vans for the local TV news stations as well as dozens of emergency vehicles. Then, of course, there were dozens of cars he assumed contained people who were just curious. He eventually pulled over, parked and walked the rest of the distance. After going a few blocks the bright blue house came into view as well as the swarms of agitated people waiting in front.

As Harold approached, Stetson met him before he could step onto the lawn. "Hey, buddy," he said looking Harold straight in the eyes. "The chief here is a real prick so brace yourself."

Harold was safely isolated inside his sorrow and knew there was nothing the police officers could say that would hurt him in any way. "I know what I'm doing, please take me to him."

There was no need to find Officer Ogden; he was marching straight at Harbinger as if he had caused this situation. "Mr. Harbinger, thank you for joining us," he said before reaching out his calloused hand. "Have you been caught up to speed, do you understand the seriousness of the situation?"

Harold studied Ogden before replying. "Yes," Harold said quietly not caring if he was heard or not. "May I speak with the animal control officers please?"

"Hold on a minute there, said Ogden. "First I need to hear the plan and make sure it's the right approach."

Harold pushed his glasses up on his nose. "It's simple, we have to round up each person in the building and put them in the animal control vans."

"That's it?" asked Ogden. "That's your high faluting plan?

Harold gathered up all his patience before he replied. "Let me make this simple for you, seems like you are having a hard time following here."

"Watch it or I'll have your ass thrown in jail for smart-mouthing an officer."

Harold scowled at him. The seconds ticked by and he remained silent.

"Well, we don't have all day, spill the plan, now," warned Ogden.

"Think about it a moment. The poles with loops on the end are the only way to capture the women and keep them at a safe distance so that they can't scratch or bite," Harold said slowly as if he were speaking to a child. Stetson stood beside him and gave him a warning nudge with his elbow. Harold looked at him briefly and from the look in Stetson's eyes he knew he had to lose the sarcasm.

Harold continued. "Once they have been captured, they can be placed in the vans and taken to a local psych hospital and put in padded rooms where they can be studied and won't be able to hurt anyone."

The group stood in stunned silence and stared at Harold. Slowly, they looked around at each other and realized the brilliance of his idea. With each inflicted person quarantined and secured it would be possible to observe and analyze, take blood samples, film their behavior and, hopefully, possibly cure each and every one of them.

A smile spread slowly on Darren Ogden's face. "Well, I do believe our expert is onto somethin."

Harold nodded in agreement, but ever somber, addressed the chief, "You do realize anyone entering the building must use the greatest caution, even with the children," he questioned. "Those women have likely taken on the roles of mother hens and are in protection mode, which means they are likely to attack. I'd send two men in at a time."

"Hold on Mr. Scientist," warned Ogden. "I'll determine who goes in, I'll decide what happens from here on out. You're just a consultant."

Harold felt his stomach rumble and he knew the source was rage. He wanted to be home alone grieving for Margaret, wanted to try a remedy for Plato, hoped to find a way to cure the wild birds and disinfect the areas at the same time. But, here he stood taking commands and insults from a cop with an enormous ego.

Ogden raised his voice and commanded two animal control workers to step forward. All four looked at each other, testing their courage and hoping to avoid this particular mission. Capturing humans that acted like zombies seemed far more ominous than any stray dog they had wrangled.

The two senior animal control workers knew it was their duty to pave the way and stepped forward. Rick, the most experienced, brought his pole forward, showing them he was ready. His pale, freckled skin blanched a shade lighter as he realized what he was about to do. "Sir, I know I have the pole and loop, but can I use a stun gun or something more to keep them at a distance?"

Ogden wiped the sweat from his face and grimaced. "You'll be fine, just think of em as big birds and everything will be okay."

Rick looked at Kyle, his cousin that he had helped get a job with animal control years before; they could pass for brothers. He was pretty certain Kyle felt terror pressing down on him too, but they stood together and faced the bright blue home. They gave each other a quick look and began the march into the mayhem they knew awaited, both ginger heads sweating in the afternoon sun.

They took the steps slowly, both aware of the clucking sounds within the building as well as garbled, mewling sounds of children. Rick reached forward and opened the front door, even though it was open just a crack, the odor of fresh bowel hit their noses. Rick also smelled a sour odor and realized it was radiating from his armpits; it was the smell of fear and he had known it many times over the years as he tackled some of the more ferocious dogs he had dragged into the van. The combination of the smells caused a sharp wave of nausea to roll over him. Sensing his discomfort, Kyle patted him on the back and urged him forward.

The scene they walked into was like a glimpse into a horror flick; the rank odor, the cluster of hostile humans in the corner, women in front guarding their fledglings, the shrillness of their cries and the claw-like hands of the women. Both men stood shoulder to shoulder and moved forward, poles in front of them, nerves wired tight. Before they had time to react, both women jumped on desks then sprang forward, claws outstretch before them and came down hard raking the faces of the men, scraping so hard they ripped through eyelids and gouged furrows down their cheeks. Both men went down on their backs, flailed and tried to use their poles to push the women off them, but the furious mother hens pushed forward with mouths open seeking flesh. Kyle felt his ear tearing from his skull and punched the woman in the face then yanked her blond braid and pulled her head back and away from his face. Her teeth continued to clamp down and seek his skin. He and Rick screamed louder than they had in their lives. The shrill screams of the men brought the other animal control officers charging into the building.

With more ease than they thought they possessed at the moment, the second wave of animal wranglers slipped the hoops on the necks of the women and pulled tight, harnessing them under control. They pulled back and started dragging the screaming women from the building. Rick and Kyle stumbled to their feet, clutching their injured faces and helping to restrain the women at the same time. *My God, these are wild cats, not birds*, thought Rick. His vision was blurry, but he kept tugging and urging and forcing until both women were inside the van and the doors were locked.

Rick felt his legs go rubbery beneath him, his face started to tingle. Kyle caught him before he hit the ground. He came to in an ambulance and saw through shredded, swollen lids a glimpse of his cousin. There was not a single inch of his face that did not burn or throb. As he reached up to touch his injuries the EMT held him back.

Kyle reached across and grabbed his hand. "Hey Bro, we did it."

After the ambulance pulled away with Rick and Kyle, the remaining spectators stared at the big blue obstacle before them. Ogden thought *Two workers left and eight children to tackle.* He looked to the remaining animal control officers and knew it was time to bolster their courage. "After that battle, taking out a bunch a kids should be a breeze," he said with forced bravery. "Just one little tot at a time and we are outta here and you can go have a cold beer."

"What you're dealing with now are basically hatchlings," explained Harold. "They have more of a group think and will stick together and we might be able to persuade them to follow us out if we offer them food."

Connie had been generous in sharing her valium and the parents were more subdued and huddled close to Harold. Connie spoke for all of them. "Yes, please feed them, they must be starved by now."

Harold knew the parents were oblivious to the real condition of their children, but there was no need to alarm them; let them believe they were still the innocent, rosy-cheeked sweethearts that had been dropped off that morning.

Harold stepped towards the building and turned to face the crowd. "Does anyone have any food with them? Something that would tempt children?" *My guess is a few raw steaks would draw them out in a hurry*, thought Harold.

"I have fruit snacks and some juice boxes I keep for emergencies, said Connie. She looked at the crowd for approval, but the parents were so overwhelmed they just wanted a leader and wanted this ordeal over. They nodded in agreement and Connie scurried to her car and returned with boxes of snacks and drinks and pushed them into Harold's arms.

Harold and the two remaining animal control workers approached the porch slowly. Even though he assumed the children would be docile, birds were unpredictable. If he had been a father he would have learned kids were equally spontaneous. He had a rough idea of what he was going to do inside the building but was prepared for anything. Knowing birds can sense fear and take advantage of it he opened the door boldly and marched straight into the middle of the room acting as fearless as possible.

He was dazzled by the colorful walls and animals painted on them. He quickly noted that all the children were huddled together in the back left corner. He scanned the room more closely and realized snakes were painted in bold bright red colors on the wall to the right. Looking back at the kids he noticed they took occasional glances at the snake paintings and shivered. "Okay, boys, stay calm and right behind me," said Harold. "Notice the snakes on the right wall? Birds are instinctively afraid of snakes and these kids, birds, whatever they are, will panic if we force them near that side of the room. Keep them to the left, okay?"

Harold looked back at them quickly and they nodded in agreement. "Follow my lead," he said as he bent down and started tossing the food a few feet in front of him. "Hey little fellas, come get your food."

He waited several minutes, but the children pulled back tighter into a safety cluster. Harold studied their movements carefully. They were presenting what he considered the frozen duckling posture. If a mother duck is approached while her hatchlings are still one to two days old they hunker down beneath her and do not move. A person could even pick up the mother, place her in a box and snatch up each and every baby and they wouldn't have a chance of escape. He knew from experience as he had rescued several mother ducks stuck in bushes surrounded by crowded parking lots or mothers trying to lead their babies to water by crossing the street. He and Margaret together had experienced the magic of saving an entire duck family by capturing mamma and babies and taking them straight to water. Watching the mom swim away with the ducklings trailing behind her in a straight line made them both cry it was so beautiful.

Still in his reverie, Harold did not see the attack coming; one of the boys, no older than five, leapt at him. Harold threw himself to the side and the child crashed into the wall behind him. Without hesitating Harold stood, grabbed the child by the ankles and hung him upside down. The boy flailed his arms and tried repeatedly to lean forward to bite Harold. Both animal control officers stood with their mouths open, speechless and unsure how to proceed.

"When dealing with a bird of prey, the most dangerous part is their talons," Harold explained. "Grab them by the ankles, dangle them in the air and they are pretty helpless." The child still squirmed and lunged towards his legs, but Harold held him at arm's length and carried him out the door. He stopped to call behind him. "Get the rest one at a time and put them in the vans."

The police moved towards Harold as he emerged and formed a solid barrier between him and the angry parents. They shielded him each step of the way to the van and blocked the parents from grabbing him.

--

The parents were so emotional and exhausted they swarmed around the two vans and demanded that their children be turned over to them. Charles Henry stepped forward. "This is an outrage! There is nothing wrong with our children," he shouted. "Hand them over!"

Chief Darren Ogden whistled as loudly as possible and all heads turned in his direction. "Your children have been infected with a deadly bacteria and they're officially in our custody," he stated with unquestionable authority. "Any attempts to touch the children will get you thrown in the slammer faster than you can say boo."

The parents shuffled their feet and Charles spat on the ground, but they stayed put.

Chapter 10 – A Bird in the Hand is Better Than Two in the Bush

"I assume you'll accompany us to the psych ward and continue to teach us about birds," said Chief Ogden. "You can drive with me if you like."

Harold reminded himself to be civil. "Sir, I'm exhausted and have matters to attend to at home. Could you give me the address and I'll be there in two hours."

Ogden pulled out a fresh piece of gum, unwrapped it and popped it into his mouth. He squinted from the sunlight and looked Harold in the face. "By now I figure you don't like me much," he said before continuing to chew. "But, the thing is, I'm realizing how much I need you."

Harold looked back towards his car and wanted more than anything to drive home and start treating Plato.

Ogden chomped at his gum like a child who was enjoying his first piece. "Now that the crowds have cleared and it is just the two of us I have a question."

I am sure you do, thought Harold.

"Mr. Harbinger we are hearing that some of the diseased are actually attempting to kill the children of others who are infected," he said before clearing his throat. "It doesn't make any sense to me or anyone else."

Harold had started thinking of the diseased as birds long before and quickly came up with an answer. "In the bird world there are some species that despise each other so much they actually kill each other's young while the parents are away from the nest."

"You don't say," said Ogden. "Why's that?"

Harold pushed his glasses up his nose. "Take the ravens and owls for example," he said. "They have a rivalry that is well known to all birders. They actually watch and wait for the parents to leave the nest, even for a minute, then kill and sometimes eat the babies. One crow can take out an entire owl clutch for the breeding season." *No wonder they call a group of crows a murder instead of a flock*, he thought to himself.

"Well, I'll be damned," said Ogden. "Never heard of anything like it, except for the nature program I watched with my wife and the male lion killed all the babies so that he could mate with the female."

Harold knew very well there was nothing similar, but people often misunderstood bird behavior. He had explained the uniqueness of birds countless times only to receive bizarre replies like the one Chief Ogden offered. He sighed. "That is not similar in the least," Harold explained. "They kill because they despise each other and have been enemies as long as they can remember. It is a powerful and dangerous instinct."

Ogden adjusted his hat on his head. "I understand that your misses has passed and that you have personal things to attend to."

Harold looked at the ground and found a small stone that he proceeded to roll around with his foot.

Ogden offered a piece of gum to Harbinger, but Harold declined. "Tell you what. Be at my office in two hours or I'm sending a squad car to your home to bring you in, got me?"

Harold looked up from the ground, "I understand." An idea came to Harold that had the potential to buy him more time and keep the police off his back. "Sir, at my lab we treat infected birds with antibiotics, you might want to attempt putting antibiotics, the strongest you can find, in the local drinking water," Harold said. "That might help prevent humans from contracting this or even cure those that already have the bacteria in their bodies. Contact the water department head and see if he can assist."

Ogden switched his gum to the other side of his mouth and continued chomping. "Well I'll be darned. You are full of surprises," he answered with a chuckle. "I'll give em a call right now. See you in two hours." He patted his round stomach as he walked to his squad car.

Plato! Harold thought as he briskly walked back to his car. *I need to get home to my boy and clean the bacteria out of his body before something happens to him.*

Chapter 11 - Oblivion

"Margaret, I am home!" sounded happily from the bedroom as Harold stepped into his house. It felt like days since he had been there, but it had been but a few hours.

"Plato, I'm home!" Harold answered sounding much younger and energetic than he felt. He was so relieved to be back with his bird that he kicked off his shoes, did not store them in their proper shelf in the closet and sprinted into the bedroom to see Plato.

"I love you, Harold. I love you, Harold," Plato chanted until Harold undid the latch and took out his best friend. Plato climbed to Harold's shoulder and nuzzled into his neck then pulled Harold's shirt forward and burrowed within and tucked himself into Harold's right armpit.

Harold felt tingles down his entire right side and felt his body relax; home and his parrot were sanctuary. "Buddy, boy! How about a treat?" Harold asked as he walked towards the kitchen.

"Plato want snack," was heard clearly through the fabric of Harold's shirt.

"What would Plato like to eat?" asked Harold.

"Plato want peanuts and raisins."

In his enthusiasm to reach his bird Harold had skipped his compulsive hand washing. To set things right he went straight to the sink and let the suds and scalding water free him of any dreadful microbes. *"Well, I guess he has enough germs already. So what if I touched him before I washed,*" thought Harold as he pulled off a paper towel and dried his hands.

"Plato, on your play stand please."

The parrot obliged and climbed out of Harold's shirt and onto his perch on the stand. Harold quickly scooped an extra helping of peanuts into the dish and shook a handful of raisins onto the stand.

Plato's eyes practically sparkled as he looked up at Harold. "Thank you, Harold."

Harold had known years before from his own research and the well-known scientific work with Alex the African Grey that these birds did a whole lot more than mimic, they could reason, count and create words on their own. The fact that Plato regurgitated niceties like "thank you" without being prompted was evidence of his intelligence.

After Plato had crunched and gulped his way through his favorite snacks Harold knew it was just a matter of seconds before he would produce a fresh dropping that he could test. True to the "food in, food out" rule, a large, dark green blob plopped onto the stand beneath Plato. Harold grabbed a swab from the nearby briefcase and slathered a thick layer onto glass slides.

Harold had expected less movement from the bacteria and even hoped to see several that were dead within the sample. What he found squashed between two pieces of glass was a thriving and growing colony of bacteria. "*How can this be? How did giving him doxycycline actually stimulate growth in the bacteria?*" He thought as he reached for a chair. He was shaky and felt a searing pain in his skull. "Perhaps a different type of antibiotic will do the trick," he thought out loud, but knew he was scrambling. He also knew he had to wipe out the bacteria in Plato's system before he could attempt to use the vaccine he had brought home.

Plato began grooming, a clear sign that he was relaxed and felt well, and Harold sat staring at him. In his line of work Harold knew just about everything there was to know about antibiotics. Ever since the creation of penicillin countless classes of antibiotics had been generated and used successfully, particular ones were more effective with birds than others. Fluoroquinolones were a group of antibiotics commonly used by avian veterinarians to cure a variety of illnesses. Harold took out paper and a pencil and started to rapidly write his thoughts. Each time he came to an idea he thought might work with Plato he found a sound reason that it could not and scratched it out, leaving deep grooves in the paper where his pencil had made its mark. Finally, he decided that Baytril, the most commonly used by veterinarians, might do the trick; that is if luck was his friend on this day.

He rifled through his brief case that contained samples and found a bottle of Baytril. It was most effective when given orally straight down a bird's throat. Harbinger understood that it was not Plato's body that was creating a resistance to the antibiotic he had given him, but the powerful bacteria itself as it had formed a resistance to doxycycline and even seemed to be thriving on it. Once a bacteria becomes resistant it becomes more deadly. "Dear God, have I just created a more deadly pathogen?" Harold asked out loud.

Harold filled a syringe, the type without a needle, similar to one used with an infant to give medication orally. He held out a jelly bean for Plato and he came to Harold happily and quickly ate the candy. Harold gently swaddled him in a soft towel and said, "Come on sweet boy, open wide." Plato did as he was asked and allowed Harold to squirt a syringe-full of Baytril down his throat. Plato made a small choking sound, but finished swallowing the medication. Harold leaned down and kissed the big, black beak. "That wasn't so bad was it, buddy?"

He unwrapped Plato and rocked him in his arms. He started to scratch the back of Plato's head when he felt Plato start struggling out of his arms. The bird looked like he was trying to swallow something that was stuck in his throat and then his face started to swell. Plato started gasping and tipping to the side, the sounds coming from his throat were of someone who was choking to death. Harold shook him gently, "Plato, Plato, breathe!"

Harold could feel Plato's heart pounding wildly and tried to maintain a hold on him as he squirmed and fluttered his wings, desperately trying to suck in air. His throat was so constricted he could no longer utter a sound; Plato seemed to be performing a pantomime of a bird suffocating to death and frantically trying to hold onto life. Just as quickly as the fluttering and gagging had begun, it was over. Plato's eyes rolled back in his head, he convulsed once and then he has perfectly still. He went limp and his head slumped to the side.

Harbinger laid Plato on the counter and started chest compressions and pried open the bird's beak and tried to breathe down his throat but it was like blowing into a fresh balloon full of resistance and impossible to inflate. "Noooo! Come on, buddy, breathe!" He massaged the bird's chest and legs hoping to get circulation going then resumed chest compressions. He heard a rib snap under the pressure and knew it was too late; his precious pet was dead.

There were no sobs, no tears only a complete feeling of emptiness. Harold heard a sharp ringing in his ears and felt disconnected from his body. He cradled Plato once again and carried him to his favorite perch where he used to sit and watch the birds through the kitchen windows. He kissed him on the head then tenderly laid Plato down on the play stand and stumbled to his bedroom.

Nobody had to tell him this was the most miserable moment of his life. No one had to explain that he was completely alone. Nobody had to even hint that he had personally killed his two favorite loved ones. He threw the messy bedding off the mattress and let his weary body collapse on his side of the bed. As he stared at the ceiling he thought of Margaret and wondered where her body was and what he should do with it and hoped there was a way Plato could be buried with her. He thought it odd that he hadn't received a call from a mortuary, but then realized her body was probably part of evidence for the police or being examined by a scientist somewhere. I am a murderer, I am a murderer, he thought as he drifted off to sleep.

--

He had just dozed off when he felt the relentless vibration of his cell in his pocket. He answered the phone, but before he could speak the police chief hammered away with his loud and irritating voice. "Darren Ogden, here. I believe you and I have an appointment Mr. Harbinger and you're late," he said without pausing for Harold's response. "I expect your butt to be in my office in a half hour or I'm sending a squad car. Over and out." A click and silence followed.

Harold felt like a robot as he pulled himself from the bed, stumbled towards the doorway, walked through the kitchen, refusing to turn his head in Plato's direction, and put his shoes on before heading out of his home. He locked the door with his key then tested it to make sure it held fast. "Mother always said there are real bad guys in the world and to always lock the door," Harold said to himself as he slowly made his way to his Prius.

He sat in the car several minutes trying to remember where he was going. When he realized it was to the police station it took many more minutes to think of how he should drive to get there. He felt like a robotic servant that was past its prime and about to be replaced, but still tried with all its rusting, computerized programming to follow orders. He started his car and headed in the direction of Officer Ogden.

--

"Ponds, lakes, rivers, swimming pools, swamp land, mud puddles," mumbled Harold as he sat in a chair inside Ogden's office. His hair was disheveled, his glasses were smudged and he had a vacant look in his eyes as if he had lost everything in the world that meant anything to him.

The chief stared at him and was stunned by the transformation that had occurred in Harold Harbinger since he had been with him two hours before. Ogden stepped out of his office for a moment and spoke with his assistant; Harold could not hear what they were discussing. Ogden reappeared with a glass of water.

Ogden offered the glass to Harold, but he sat still speaking gibberish about water sources, antibiotics and dead birds. Ogden cleared his throat. "Son, I think you better have this drink seems like you've got heat stroke or somethin'."

Harold looked up and noticed Ogden standing in front of him. "Could I please have that water?"

Ogden softened his voice. "This is for you and there's more where that came from."

Harold drank the water quickly and asked for more. Ogden motioned to his assistant and she came in with a cold can of soda. After Harold had finished his drink and the sugar was working in his system speaking became easier. "Did you get it in the water? Did you?" Harold asked as he leaned forward with a panicked expression in his eyes. "Are antibiotics in the water already?"

"Don't worry, less than an hour ago antibiotics, powerful ones at that, were added to the local water supply and the info will be on the news tonight just in case there are any folks allergic to antibiotics." Ogden answered with a smile.

"Nooo! You can't!" Harold shouted as he stood from his chair.

At his shout two police officers dashed into Ogden's office, but he made a gesture with his hands for them to stay put and not touch Harold. Ogden sat on the corner of his desk. "Son, you are the one who suggested we put antibiotics in the water to help prevent the people from catching this nasty bug."

"Plato is dead," Harold said as though everyone in the room would understand the significance.

Ogden scratched his head. "You are not making any sense Mr. Harbinger, mind clarifying for all of us."

Harold stood up, walked over to Ogden and whispered in his ear. "Plato is dead."

Ogden looked at his men and gestured for them to step forward. "We need a psych eval in here pronto."

Harold ignored the chief and examined the items on Ogden's desk one by one, pausing the longest to study the framed family photo.

Ogden put his arm around Harold's waist and urged him to sit back down. When Harold was settled in his chair Ogden leaned forward. "What happened to you after you left the daycare?" asked Ogden with real concern for the first time. "Who is Plato, does he have something to do with why you aren't acting like the Mr. Harbinger you were a few hours ago?"

"He was my son, well, the closest thing I was ever going to have to a son and I killed him."

Ogden instinctively rested his hand on his gun holster. "Harold, are you saying you murdered your son?"

"I am a murderer, you guessed it. First Margaret, then Plato," Harold said as hot tears started coursing down his cheeks. Ogden's officers stepped in closer both pulling out their revolvers, but Ogden held them back.

Harold began sobbing not caring that snot ran onto his upper lip or that he was babbling like an infant in front of the Chief of Police. "If I hadn't brought the germs home they would still be alive," he wailed then looked pleadingly into Ogden's eyes. "They are dead aren't they and they're not coming back." Harold fell to his knees on the carpet then rolled into a ball sobbing and wailing until the official psychiatrist for the police department came into the room and gave him an injection in his arm that eased him into sleep within seconds.

--

Harold awoke hours later in a cell on a cot with Bill Stetson seated across the room in a chair. When Stetson saw Harold stir he came over and sat on the cot. Although he was disoriented Harbinger was relieved to see Stetson. He had a few seconds of peace and then the reality that Plato was dead slammed into him. The tears were coursing freely again and Stetson let Harold get to his story in his own time. After several minutes Harold cleaned his face and glasses and looked up at Stetson.

Harold cleared his throat. "It hurts so much, so much it doesn't seem real."

Stetson patted Harold's leg. "I think the best thing you can do right now is tell me what happened. If you're ready to talk I can get Ogden back in here too."

"Let's do without Ogden for now," said Harold as he tried to sit up; the medication was still wearing off and he felt a bit dizzy. "Plato is dead." Seeing that Stetson did not recall who Plato was he elaborated. "My parrot, Plato, is dead and I killed him."

Stetson scratched his head and let out a long sigh, the usual smell of coffee present in his breath. "Why in the world did you kill your pet?"

"It wasn't on purpose. He was infected with the bacteria and was a carrier, probably the one who got Margaret sick and the reason she died," Harold explained. "I gave him some very powerful antibiotics trying to clean the bugs out of his system and he must have had an allergic reaction to it."

"Do you realize that from the things you said in the chief's office he thinks you murdered someone?" asked Stetson.

Harold sat quietly for a long time before answering. "Bill, I hardly remember being in Ogden's office. If he'd like I can give him a full statement now and explain myself. I'm more calm and thinking clearly."

"That would be good, in fact, that would be perfect because they still need your help," Stetson said. "There are new problems to deal with."

--

After Harold explained what had happened to his parrot and how using antibiotics might be killing birds at that very moment, Ogden seemed ready to listen to Harbinger once again.

Ogden opened a fresh piece of gum and popped it in his mouth. While he chewed and let it soften in his mouth he started the inquisition all over again. "Why in the world didn't you tell me it was a bird to begin with? We were all thinking you were a serial killer or something."

"It doesn't matter now, what matters is that we do not continue with the antibiotics because it could kill too many birds," explained Harbinger. "For all I know it could kill humans who are infected with the bacteria as well."

Ogden shook his head, "It's already too late. Reports are coming in that birds are dying and then coming back to life and trying with a vengeance to peck out the eyes of any human they get close to."

"God help us all," said Harold. "How is the police department or whoever is in charge dealing with the birds that are doing this?"

"They are harder than hell to kill so far," Ogden explained. "The only way to stop them is to smash them to mush or cut their heads off."

Harold felt his stomach roll over and barely made it to the waste basket in the chief's office before the vomit emptied out of him. Wretch after wretch he emptied every last drop of soda pop, undigested food and acid. He stared uncomprehendingly at the drool that generously flowed from his mouth and dripped into the basket.

The room was devastatingly quiet until Bill Stetson kneeled beside him and applied a cool, wet cloth to his forehead. "Buddy, do you feel up to taking a seat?" he asked as he guided Harold back to his chair.

Harold nodded, but did not have the presence of mind to speak. He stared at his shoes and wiped the drool from his lips with the back of his hands. "Are you telling me that these are wild birds attacking or do they appear to be pet birds that drank tap water?" Harold asked as he slowly raised his gaze to meet Ogden's.

Chief Ogden had to think a while before answering then still had to refer to notes on his desk. "They are all the same to me, I'm not a bird type of person," Ogden said as he stared at the notes. "This says some black birds, some with bright colors, I'm not sure if they are wild or not because the water people also put antibiotics in the local ponds and other small bodies of water."

Harold Harbinger sat perfectly still. He wanted to remember this moment, this exact speck of time when his world came to an end. This was precisely the nanosecond when his soul emptied out and there was nothing left because he knew it was the end of birds on the planet he called earth. Yes, he could continue to breathe, speak, eat and walk, but without all the feathered, glorious creatures in his life he was finished.

"Mr. Harbinger?" Ogden waited patiently for a few moments, but the urgency of the situation forced him to speak again. "Mr. Harbinger, we need your help."

"Let me guess. You need my help finding the easiest way to kill all the birds," Harold said blankly. "You don't even need another "psych consult" to get answers from me. What do you need to know, exactly?"

Over the next hour Ogden, his team, and Stetson, who had been reinstated due to the circumstances, listened intently while Harbinger discussed the bird populations in the area, their sleeping habits and the best way to capture all of them while they were in roost mode during the night. He did it willingly, void of emotion or care. He understood on a scientific level that although birds had inhabited the planet since the day of the dinosaurs and were, in fact, considered modern-day dinosaurs by many a scientist, their time on the planet had come to an end because of one rogue bacteria, one that he had managed to bring home from Avetech and share with the most precious creatures in the world – Margaret and all the birds he could think of.

Under his direction the National Guard, wildlife officials and hordes of animal control officers, police and citizen volunteers proceeded to roosting sites of starlings and sparrows first. They had long been considered garbage birds by the general population and were easy targets for their first attempt at annihilation. Because it was pitch black and all birds were deep in a stupor of roosting with their knees locked onto branches so they would not fall and bodies in a mild form of hibernation, they would not struggle or fly away. Massive canvas bags with plastic inner lining were thrown over trees and bushes where they slept and then cinched tight.

"Birds have air sacs all over their bodies in addition to lungs," explained Harold. "They can absorb, if you will, gases at a much faster rate." He looked around the enormous group to make sure they all understood. "Just remember the old saying 'like a canary in a gold mine' and you'll get it." He told them a brand new non-stick pan heated for the first time emitted a gas that killed birds instantly if they were in the room near the pan while it was heating. Countless bird owners each year lost beloved pets to their new pans and felt pangs of guilt because of it. Harbinger told them something as simple as fingernail polish remover could kill a bird if they breathed in enough of it.

Ogden stepped forward. "Let me get this straight, if we have the birds inside the bags they will likely suffocate before sunrise, but if we add a container of gasoline or another toxic substance they will die right away?"

"That is correct," Harbinger answered. "Tie the bags tight with rags soaked in gasoline inside so that the birds will go quickly in their sleep." He adored sparrows for their tenacity, ability to survive in cities and the rural areas, he was charmed by their soft, brown feathers and chirps. They were some of the kinder birds, but they were also misunderstood and underappreciated.

Margaret had worked at home writing articles for national publications dedicated to birding as well as contributing to books on behaviors of North American birds. Because she worked from home she was able to raise orphan sparrows and starlings. She was not a licensed bird rehabber and didn't need to be if she just worked with birds that were not protected. Consequently, over the years Harold had grown to love the tiny featherless sparrows that arrived each spring and cherished his time feeding them and helping Margaret when he was home after work. The Starlings were usually so hardy and boisterous he especially enjoyed having them in the home. Margaret taught all of them to feed themselves when they were older, showed them how to forage in the yard for insects and gradually released them and continued to supplement their food supply after they had left her care.

Even with his history with sparrows and starlings he found it impossible to raise any emotion or feeling at the prospect of killing thousands of birds in one night. The cold night air clung to him and he pulled the police jacket tighter around his shoulders. He could effectively put up a solid barrier in his mind that would not allow him to think of Margaret, Plato or any other bird. He was performing as a citizen of the world attempting to save countless humans from being attacked or even killed by wild birds.

His rational brain told him it was inevitable that they should be killed and he proceeded in a soldier-like fashion dispensing information that would kill thousands of birds that very night. His emotional brain told him how wrong it was, screamed at him in fact that birds should be saved no matter what. But, he would lose that argument with authorities not only because he was outnumbered but because birds were turning and were attacking humans and humans always came first.

He felt the familiar vibration in his pocket and wondered who would be calling at 2 a.m. He pulled his phone from his pocket and saw Avetech displayed on the screen. "Who in the world would be calling at this hour?" he said before answering the phone. "Harbinger here."

"Harold, this is Davis and I have something very important to speak with you about regarding the birds in the lab."

Harold paused before replying. Davis was the youngest on the team. He had been something of a child genius, gone to college at a young age and had a PhD in Ornithology by the time he was twenty. He had only worked at Avetech a little over a year and was full of enthusiasm. Harold's passion for birds was only exceeded by that of Davis. "What is it?" Harold asked.

"It's Harriet, the pionus parrot," Davis blurted. "The bacteria in her droppings . . . "

Harold shut him down. "I know all about the bacteria, I assume all the birds in the lab have it. No matter what you do make sure you wear your biohazard suit and wash thoroughly before going home." Ogden waved Harbinger over. "I have to go, next time call at a decent hour." Harold hung up his phone and walked to Ogden to give the final orders.

Harold stared at the canvas bags securely fastened around several bushes and small pine trees. He knew inside hundreds, perhaps thousands of sparrows roosted securely, unaware of the doom that hovered in their futures. By now several had likely succumbed to the fumes and were dead or on their way. They had decided earlier in the night that while the birds were dying or dead inside the bags they would set them ablaze to totally erase the bacteria and avoid having to deal with diseased bodies in the morning. Charred remains would be easier to dispose of and would cause less fear among the many who would be on clean up duty.

He stepped forward to instruct the National Guard employees on lighting the entire row of bushes on fire but felt the insistent buzzing vibration in his pocket. When he looked at the caller identification it was Avetech again. *Probably that damn blonde Davis kid again*, he thought. *Why in the world is he being so persistent? He reminds me of how I used to be when I started working at Avetech.*

Harold was entirely encased in numbness inside and out and no longer cared about Avetech or the birds wrapped within the death traps before him. He stepped forward and raised his voice, "Now that they are likely succumbing to the fumes of the gasoline and are starting to die, let's burn them quickly before they have a chance to turn and attack," spoke Harold with more forcefulness than he had known in his lifetime. "Get your torches men and light them up!"

Within seconds National Guard employees torched the canvas bags and crackling sounds and smoke began to fill the air. As the canvas bags were consumed by flames gaps began to appear in the fabric. Tiny brown birds began darting out and torpedoing straight at the workers, their sharp yellow beaks and entire bodies aimed at the men and women who huddled together watching the flames. They shrieked and chattered angrily and became magnificent darts soaring through the night sky. Their vision was clear as the fires illuminated the air and made it possible to see well enough to force their small bodies straight into eye sockets that stared in horror.

One woman worker screamed and tugged at the bird that was lodged deep within her eye, but she could not dislodge it. It scratched with its tiny feet at her cheek, drawing blood in tidy, even rows and fluttered its wings as if it was trying to beat her to death with its feathers. She managed to dislodge it a bit at a time and when it was finally within her grasp, writhing and pecking with all its might, she wrapped her fingers around it tight and began to squeeze until her perfectly polished nails, in the season's hottest color, blaze red, sunk into its body melding with shattered bones, organs and vibrant scarlet blood. She hurled its remains to the ground and placed her shoe over its head, stepped down hard and heard a satisfying pop as its skull exploded.

As the multitudes of birds turned into cinders, the escapees became furious missiles aimed at eyeballs and attacked again and again, never missing their targets, giving their lives to take out the vision of their assailants. With each eye they destroyed, their small bodies were eventually tugged free from the eye sockets and then smashed inside angry fists or beneath sturdy boots. All that remained of each bird was a feathery, gooey, bloody mess that would have to be cleaned away with a powerful hose the next morning. Within an hour all the birds targeted were dead, several people on the kill team were blinded, some in just one eye, and not one soul who witnessed the carnage would ever be the same, Harold most of all.

Watching the horrendous scene glimpses of the old Harold began to surface and he felt a deep ache in his heart for the tiny sparrows. However, as soon as he allowed the feelings to enter, he shut them down; there was no way he could lead this massive team and allow himself to become personally concerned.

As the team began the cleanup of the area and gathered the charred remains of bushes, bags and birds, Harold found himself moving further from the setting until he was on the periphery simply observing. He was fascinated that there was so much emotion at play, yet he felt none. The workers had been trained through the toughing process of boot camp, but there were many among them who were weeping both quietly to themselves and some openly at the losses they had seen. He listened carefully and learned that many of the volunteers also loved birds and felt an immense loss or felt sick to know they had been part of it. But, then again, there were those who were burning up with anger over the attacks they had witnessed or received. Never in their lives had they imagined such tiny birds attacking with such ferocity that they could destroy a human's eyeballs.

Harold's backside was growing numb because he had sat on it so long as he leaned against the guardrail watching the mob massacre the song birds. As he was standing to establish circulation in his legs again he felt the familiar vibration of his cell phone. Just as he suspected, it was Avetech again. Speaking to any employee who worked with birds was the very last thing he wanted at this moment in his life and he put the phone back in his pocket. He heard a beep a minute later and knew there was a voice message waiting for him.

Chapter 12 – The Undoing

Harold smelled of smoke and he reeked of his own sweat, the particular sour smelling sweat that the body produces during times of high stress and fear. On the drive home inside his tiny Prius the odors were almost suffocating so he drove with the windows down. As he turned into his neighborhood he noticed how entirely quiet it was. There were no neighbors mowing lawns, trimming hedges or sitting on the porches. There were no other cars pulling in or out of driveways. As he drove closer to his home he did hear the neighbor's dog, but his bark had more of an intense, desperate sound. All the clues added up instantly and Harold realized most or all of his neighbors were dead and that he was driving through something of a ghost town. He wondered who would feed the dog, but just as quickly as his concern had bloomed he cut it away just as he had done with all his emotions through the night.

He had worked through the darkness along with the brigades of bird-killers and was more tired than he thought humanly possible; he was filthy and starving too. As he pulled into his driveway he felt relief and the thought of throwing himself into the bed and sleeping for days was all he wanted. Sleep brought oblivion and the only real escape from what was actually transpiring where he lived and in the adjoining towns.

He turned off the car, gathered his few belongings and climbed out of the Prius making sure to lock it as he walked away and turned back to click the lock button on his key one more time. He mounted the front steps, unlocked the front door and stepped inside. The stillness and perfect quiet of his home hit him. He anticipated the usual "Margaret, I am home" but there was nothing but silence. He was so eager to see Plato that he couldn't wait for the customary call and shouted out, "Plato, I am home!" The second the last syllable left his mouth stinging tears came to his eyes. He stood still in the entrance hearing nothing but his breathing and the sound of his tears as they splattered one at a time on the wood floor. Minutes went by with his head drooped to his chest and tears trickling away. Finally, Harold found the fortitude to push back his emotions and swallowed his sadness. "Harold, Plato is dead, remember?" he said out loud.

His parrot had been with him so many years and his antics and constant chatter had filled the home with noise, laughter and love. Harold had never in all his life felt so alone and miserable. He didn't have the courage to walk into the kitchen just yet; he was not ready to see Plato's dead body. His glasses were streaked with salty tracks from his tears. He took them off, pulled his inner shirt free and rubbed his lenses. The glasses were a bit cleaner, but some spots were worse as they were now smudged with ashes as well.

Harold took a deep breath and calmed his breathing. *I think I will bury him under the bright pink rose bush in the corner of the yard that was Margaret's favorite. She would like that.* He thought as he took off his shoes and put them on the shoe rack. It was inevitable and Harold knew time wasn't going to make it any easier. He had to face the body of Plato and prepare to bury him. *I will cut most of the roses that are at full bloom and put them in the grave with him.* A sad smile appeared on his lips as he walked into the kitchen. When he reached the play stand and found it empty he stood frozen and speechless. *Wait, am I wrong? Did I put his body somewhere else?* He thought as he turned to look around the room. The day before had been a misery and the night was truly a nightmare and he wasn't thinking perfectly clearly, but even so, he knew the play stand was where he had left the body.

"Margaret, I am home!" sounded loudly behind him somewhat garbled, but still clearly Plato. Every hair on his arms stood up and he felt the hairs at the nape of his neck rise with them. *Terror, this is what terror feels like.* He didn't want to turn around and see what his bird had become. All the workers from last night were calling the birds that had turned flying zombies, but he didn't want to see Plato with filmy grey eyes and a deathly pallor.

Harold switched into the scientist mode and tried to rationally think through the situation. "Harold, I love you. I love you, Harold" Plato chimed from somewhere above and behind Harold.

He has taken a high spot for perching to watch for prey and have the upper hand, thought Harold as he tried to think of what to do. He turned slowly and looked up. There on top of the cupboards, in gargoyle fashion, perched Plato on the corner of the upper cupboards. His eyes were pure foggy white and the already grey skin of his face hung in waddles on both sides of his face. His feathers were ruffled and raised to their fullest height around his neck, a sure sign of a bird that was threatened or ready to attack.

Harold took a step back. "Hey, buddy, how about a treat? Would Plato like some raisins?"

Plato did not answer; he stared at Harold with his dead eyes then fluttered to the counter three short feet from Harold.

"Here, pal, have some raisins," Harold said as he opened the cupboard grabbed a handful, spilling half of them onto the floor and piled what remained on the counter.

Plato didn't even look at the treats as he started walking towards Harold. The tap, tap, tapping of his claws on the granite counter echoed through the kitchen and silent home. Harold stepped back towards the sink until his back was to the counter and he could move no further. With no warning Plato flew at his face, claws outstretched and beak wide open. He clamped onto Harold's face with his claws and bit hard into Harold's nose with his powerful, thick beak. Harold screamed as Plato started beating his head with his wings. Each blow landed directly on his ears and the sound was deafening and painful. Harold put both hands on Plato and pulled with all his strength, but Plato held on tight and clamped his beak deeper into Harold's nose. The bird reached up repeatedly with his feet towards Harold's eyes, trying with all his might to scratch them out, but his glasses, with their thick lenses, were the only thing protecting his eyes.

In a desperate move Harold lunged forward and smashed his face into the counter squashing Plato between his head and the hard counter, hurting the bird and dislodging him in one move. Plato squawked loudly as his bones broke and he lost hold of Harold's face. Knowing he might only have seconds to get away, Harold sprinted towards the bedroom, what remained of his nose bobbing as he ran. He knew there was no time to close and lock the door, but made it to his bedroom closet, shut the door and leaned against it. Safe in the darkness behind the thick wooden door he slumped against the door and let his body slide to the carpet. He reached up and felt for a flannel shirt knowing it would be soft and sturdy enough to hold against his ravaged face. Even in the darkness it was easy to find and he pulled it pressed it into the deep grooves allowing time for it to soak up blood then used it to prop up the remnants of his nose.

Just outside his sanctuary he heard Plato walk across the tile floor. Each step produced a rapping sound as his claws made contact with the tile there was also a dragging sound that he assumed was a broken wing tagging along behind the parrot. Harold scrunched down on the carpet and flattened his body as much as possible so that he could look through the one inch gap under the door. Back and forth went the grey feet and a broken wing with a compound fracture, the jagged bone poking out. Each step of the way his claws clicked on the tile and he mumbled, "Harold, I love you," his words becoming a chant as he continued with his death march.

It was the most morbid moment of Harold's entire life and although he had loved the bird with everything he had yesterday, *or was it the day before?* So much had happened he had lost track of time. He had loved him, but propping up what was left of his nose and wiping his bleeding face on the flannel shirt, what he felt was hatred. Harold couldn't remember the last time he had felt hate. He had a job he loved, a woman he adored and the best pet he could have asked for. What he had now was nothing but a murderous parrot, a city with bird corpses and a mangled face.

Harold turned his back once again, and slumped against the door. He pulled his cell phone out of his pocket and with its light he dialed the only person who could help. After several rings he got the voice mail of Bill Stetson. "Bill, this is Harold and it's an emergency, please call me."

He held the phone and stared at it as if it was enough to get Bill to return his call. The minutes ticked by and Harold redialed, but once again, Bill did not answer. Harold noticed the voice mail message and pressed it. "Hello, Mr. Harbinger, this is Davis, again. As I mentioned I have discovered something amazing in Harriet's droppings. This might change everything, um, please call me as soon as possible."

The tiniest glimpse of hope started to warm inside Harold. Right at that moment the cell rang and Harold answered quickly, "Davis?"

"Um, no, this is Bill," Stetson said with a sleep-deprived voice. "What's the big emergency?"

"Bill, listen carefully because the way you respond to this situation is going to impact both of us."

During the next few minutes Harold laid out a plan that Stetson was supposed to follow to the smallest detail or, he was warned, he too was going to have to make an appointment with a plastic surgeon in the near future.

After hanging up he felt the darkness and smallness of the closet squeezing in on him while he listened intently to every sound Plato made. Presently, there was not a sound to be heard coming from his bathroom. He knew Plato and parrots well enough to know he had not left; he was simply biding his time waiting for the right moment to catch Harold off guard. After several minutes of silence, Harold heard a soft fluttering sound accompanied by a scratching noise, both sounding like they were right against the closet door. Harold reached up and put his hand on the door handle and felt the slightest movement and knew Plato was trying to turn the handle. *There is no way in hell that monster is going to open this door with just two feet and a broken wing.* Still he held tight to the handle and refused to let it budge. "Let go, Plato, bad bird!" Harold yelled. Plato plopped to the floor and continued his march. "Harold, I love you."

Trying to outmaneuver the bird, Harold reached up and fumbled through the clothing and hangers until he found a simple wire hanger, the type the dry cleaners hung his freshly laundered shirt upon. He pulled it down and began to bend it into a long hook in hopes of reaching under the door and snagging Plato as he kept his vigil in front of the door.

When the hanger was ready Harold lay on his stomach and turned his head to the side. His nose ached with a vengeance, but he had to see exactly where Plato was. Squinting through the opening he could see that perhaps six inches from the door Plato stood and occasionally turned directions as if he was scanning the area for intruders. As quietly as he could Harold slid the hanger towards Plato intent on hooking both his feet and dragging him under the door far enough that his legs would be pinned and he would put up less of a fight when Stetson arrived.

Although those were his intentions, Plato was thinking ahead of him again. He saw the wire snaking out from under the closet door and grasped it firmly with his beak and started to tug it towards him. Harold held on tight, but the wire slipped from his grasp and he heard a clanking sound as Plato tossed it across the room.

As Harold stared under the door for signs of Plato's return to his post he was startled when the bird's head suddenly appeared in view right in the one inch frame under the door. His head was tilted sideways so a waddle of wrinkled skin plopped onto the tile. With white eyes and skin sagging, his black tongue slithered out and licked the blood off his beak. "How's about a kiss baby?"

Harold felt his face flush hot with fury knowing the zombie bird was savoring his blood. He was so horrified by the evil that had claimed Plato, his body shuddered, which was something he had heard about, but thought only happened in fiction or the movies. He could not comprehend how in the world it could be the same bird he had hand-fed and raised from infancy and the very bird that was like a child to him. It didn't take long for him to calm himself and accept the fact that it truly was not Plato any longer, it was a zombie or whatever they were considering the birds that had died and turned. There was no love for this creature in his heart; all he felt was a hot liquid hate and couldn't wait for Stetson to end this sick charade.

Harold checked his cell to see the time and wondered how long ago he had placed the call to Stetson. He was wishing he had taken note of the time when he heard muffled sounds coming from the front room. As the sounds became more audible he realized it was Stetson marching through his home straight towards the bathroom. As he got closer Plato began squawking and making threatening sounds as if he was trying to protect Harold. *How messed up is this situation going to get? He wants to kill me, but nobody else has the right?* Thought Harold to himself. *Or perhaps Plato is just warming up for his attack against Stetson.*

Either way, Plato had a lot of surprises coming right at him. Although Harold could not see what was happening he saw it clearly in his mind and assumed Bill had carried out orders down to the last detail. Stetson stomped into the bathroom without fear, fully padded in a bullet proof vest as well as a police protective, bullet proof helmet complete with a facial shield. He would also have his pistol out with the safety off. Harold heard a shuffling of feet from Stetson, fluttering of wings, squawking, shrieking and screaming from Plato. He plugged his ears and didn't want to hear the final sound he was waiting for.

Although his index fingers were plunged deep into his ears he heard the pistol fire and then a loud thud.

Several seconds later the closet door was slowly opened. Harold saw Stetson as he turned the handle with one hand and removed his helmet with the other. "Hey, Buddy Boy, I think you better stay in there a minute while I clean up this mess," said Stetson in a fatherly tone. "I really don't want you to see him this way."

Harold pushed the door shut without a word and leaned against the closet door and listened to Stetson wiping and sweeping and then, surprisingly, speaking gently to the dead bird. He could only hear bits of the words through the door, but the snippets that met his ears were sweet in deed. "I'm so sorry little guy. I know Harold loved you more than anything and this wasn't your fault."

Stetson tapped gently on the door. "You can come out now, Harold."

Harold reluctantly left the safety of the closet and emerged in the sunny bathroom where Stetson stood with a towel in his arms. On his second glance Harold realized Plato was wrapped within so that Harold would not have to see him.

Harold looked Stetson straight in the eyes. "Thank you. What you did couldn't have been easy, but it certainly was necessary."

"Anything for a friend," answered Stetson without the slightest delay.

Harold stood still and thought a moment and realized Stetson was a friend, a true one at that. All he could do was nod in agreement. "Bill, would you mind sticking around for one more thing?"

"Whatever you need."

Together they went into the backyard and Harold retrieved a shovel from the shed and was startled and disgusted all over again when he saw the Johansens. He knew eventually he would have to report their deaths or find a way to move the bodies to their own yard, but for now a shovel was all he could handle. For a good half hour he and Stetson dug a deep hole near the bright pink rose bushes in the back corner where Plato had spent so many happy hours with Margaret. Harold and Stetson took turns digging, careful not to disturb the roots of the bushes while they made a grave. When it was Stetson's turn to dig, Harold went around the yard and cut the most beautiful of all the roses and piled them high beside the grave.

"Bill, I think we need the hole a bit deeper before I can put Plato in there."

"Well, deeper it will be," said Stetson with a sad smile.

When the hole was as deep as it was going to be, Harold began placing the loveliest roses in the bottom. Occasionally Bill plucked one from the pile and put it in the grave and helped arrange the flowers so that they appeared to be a beautiful bed waiting for the prince of all birds to take his final rest. The finished sight was spectacular and brought tears to Bill's eyes. "I'm so sorry, Harold, so very sorry," he said. "You loved him so much and I know you blame yourself, but sometimes in life chaos just happens and germs become part a the mix and people and creatures you love die."

Harold hadn't spoken for several minutes and looked thoughtfully at Stetson. He had cried so much during the past few days and was so tired from the night of murdering starlings and sparrows he had no strength to reply.

Stetson gently unfolded the towel and brought out what remained of Plato's body and placed it in the grave. Harold closed his eyes and began mumbling a prayer that Stetson could not understand. With Plato nestled among the flowers Harold reached out and put the remaining roses on top of him so that every inch of the parrot was covered in peach, yellow, red, maroon, orange and white fragrant petals. It was a proper resting place for a bird that had been loved dearly and gave so much in return during his life.

Together they used their hands and filled the grave with dirt. "I don't want to live in a world without birds. I have loved them ever since I was a tiny boy. They hold the magic, the real magic on this planet," Harold said as he worked. He was quiet for a moment then continued. "You know, as Plato's body decomposes the nutrients from his remains will add to the soil and make the rose bush bloom more beautifully than ever," explained Harbinger. "Margaret used to bury any wild bird that did not survive under her rose bushes. She said it was a way for them to live again through the flowers."

"I do believe that's the most beautiful thing I've heard in a long time," replied Stetson. He paused a moment and then asked. "You a fan of Emily Dickinson?"

"I can't say I'm very familiar with her work, but I have heard enough to know she was a talented writer," answered Harold.

Stetson continued. "My mother was crazy for her poetry and had several of her favorite poems memorized. When life seemed tough and my mom didn't want me to give up hope she'd recite her favorite Emily Dickinson poem to me. I do believe it goes 'Hope is the thing with feathers that perches in the soul and sings a tune without the words and never stops at all.' There is more to it, but that's the most important part of the poem."

Harold looked at his new friend and found himself feeling the smallest glimpse of hope. He also realized he had misjudged a highway patrolman and thought he could never appreciate the finer things in life like poetry. "That was lovely, Bill. Thank you."

There was a still pause where they both looked at each other, countless thoughts circling through their minds. Bill spoke first. "Well, you look beat to hell. How about you clean up, we get you to a doctor and then you go out for a cup of coffee with me?" Bill asked, but assumed the answer would be a prompt no.

Harold sat on the cement bench beside the bird bath and looked at Plato's grave. There was nothing here for him now, nobody to love and he felt certain within days all the birds in the world would be wiped out. "I appreciate the offer, really I do, but not right now, not today, and probably not for a long time."

"I thought so," replied Stetson. "How about you try and get some sleep and a shower; you stink to high heaven. I'll go home and do the same. Talk with you soon." Bill leaned the shovel against the house as he walked towards the street and didn't look back.

Chapter 13 – Resurrection

After Stetson left and Harold was alone in his backyard and the weight of his grieving was settling over him, he decided to focus on the possibilities of a cure that Davis had hinted at in his message. He picked up his cell and dialed Avetech and asked for Davis Jensen.

"Davis here," answered the young researcher.

"Davis, this is Harold Harbinger, you called to tell me something about Harriet."

"Sir, it's her droppings, the bacteria have started to die," he said with pure optimism in his voice. "In fact, as of an hour ago, there were only a few alive under the scope and moving slowly."

"That's amazing, what exactly are you saying," asked Harold as he gingerly touched his nose and nudged the injured chunk back into place. "Did you give her a new antibiotic or medication I don't know about?

"Sir, don't think me naïve or unsophisticated, but I have always trusted my grandmother," he said a bit shyly. "And, she said not to trust modern medicine, that nature held a cure for almost anything."

Harbinger thought for a moment. "Continue, you aren't making any sense." Harold's face was throbbing and he was running out of patience.

"Well, sir, um, I called my grandmother and she recommended that I take all the seed away from the birds and feed them only fruits high in vitamin C as well as forcing them to eat garlic.'"

"That is ridiculous," retorted Harbinger.

"Sir, I know it sounds like a childish approach, but that is exactly what I did with Harriet a few days ago," he explained. "It worked so well I started the vitamin C and garlic with the other birds yesterday. My guess is when I look at their droppings under the scope I will see dying bacteria, at least I hope so."

Harold sat quietly wondering just how to respond. "Give me just a second to process this."

While Harbinger sat, a woodpecker returned to his yard, landed high in the tree top and began pounding away at the bark just as it had done days before. "Davis, keep up the good work and report to me this afternoon."

He hung up without a goodbye and then sat watching the woodpecker and realized it was a species that ate high in the treetops, roosted in a hollowed out cavity in a tree and was likely to avoid the bacteria a lot of the other birds were in contact with. He was stunned at his brilliant young associate and his discovery and at seeing a spectacular bird in his own yard. The spark of hope within him Stetson had started with a simple poem began to burn a bit brighter.

Harold practically ran into the house, showered quickly and dressed before heading to the hospital. In the emergency room they insisted that his face was so badly disfigured he should have a plastic surgeon attach the dangling portion of his nose and repair the gouges in his face, but he opted for the resident putting in stitches. His mind was full of fresh ideas on how to wipe out the bacteria on the ground as well as adding vitamin C to the drinking water and natural sources of water in the area and surrounding towns. Those two steps just might be enough to save the wild birds that remained. He had to see Darren Ogden and stop him before more wild birds were killed.

Chapter 14 – Flight

The planet earth is a dynamic sphere in the universe. The dinosaurs had their millions of years to reign, primitive man and furry beasts rose to rule the planet and one simple bacteria almost destroyed all feathered creatures and a huge chunk of mankind. In the end the solution had been simple; vitamins in water, disinfecting areas with bird droppings and giving supplements to people and feathered creatures in the early stages of acquiring the bacteria were basic steps that saved them. Unfortunately, thousands of birds died before they could treat them and hundreds of humans lost their lives. But, twelve months later life marched on, businesses continued to run, people bought groceries, worked out at the gym, frolicked in the golden sun of California and some were starting to forget how horrendous the zombie flock epidemic had been. Harold alone would remember every detail and if there were moments when his memory failed him, his journal was there to promptly remind him of the massacres and mayhem and the framed photographs of his wife and parrot adorned the mantles and table tops of his home.

It was hard to believe an entire year had passed and that the addition to his home went so smoothly. The Florida room was complete and full of bird cages. It was sunny and glorious and potted rose bushes thrived in every corner and spare area of the room. Each cage was huge and contained a nesting box and a breeding pair of parrots. Harriet the pionus from Avetech and a male as well as their three chicks were part of the menagerie. Countless varieties of conures, parrots and exotic birds filled the massive room with boisterous, happy sounds. Babies squawked for their parents to feed them and from all appearances it was paradise for Harold.

Davis and Harold strolled through the room enjoying the morning light and sipping their tea. "I'm thrilled at the progress you've made in such a short period of time," said Davis.

"My mother always said when I locked my mind on an idea I didn't let go," explained Harbinger. "But, Avetech deserves a lot of the credit for funding my project and helping me acquire these spectacular birds."

Davis swizzled the last bit of tea in his cup before swallowing. "You know don't you how lucky we are?"

"How is that?" asked Harold as he started his morning routine of providing clean water for each cage. While he washed dishes he looked up at Davis.

"Come on, do I have to spell it all out? I guess I do," he said as he joined Harold in watering and feeding the birds. "We came so close to losing all the birds in the world, but my grandma, a simple woman in her late eighties, turned it all around."

A thoughtful expression came across Harold's face. "She did, didn't she. I'm so sorry she died before I got to meet her."

Davis teared up for a moment and found it difficult to speak. "I'm just thankful she went quietly in her sleep and that she lived such a long life," he said as he wiped one stray tear. "I have to look at what she helped save and believe in what we still have to look forward to.

My grandmother raised me and taught me to love birds, because of her I chose my path as an ornithologist. And, because of that we were able to work together to find a cure."

"Son, I would not for one moment attempt to own any part of the solution," Harbinger said as he picked up a watering can and poured its contents into a planter that contained a drooping rose bush. "It was all you."

Davis worked his way around the room humming and stopping to scratch heads that pressed against the bars. He pulled peanuts from his pockets and offered them to the waiting birds. "Sir?"

"When are you going to stop calling me Sir?" asked Harbinger. "Aren't we friends by now? Call me Harold please."

"Harold, do you think people are ready to forgive and love birds again?"

"I hope so, I truly do. Considering the number of volunteers who come through this place each week my guess is eventually people will start putting bird feeders back up and will pick up their binoculars again just trying to get a glimpse of a favorite bird."

After they finished in the breeding room they headed into the kitchen where Harold had buckets of tiny baby sparrows and cages of starling fledglings on the counters. Both species of birds were hardy and had survived so much over the years, Harold was not surprised flocks were returning to the area, so many in fact that occasionally babies were found that needed help just like before when Margaret was alive and raising them.

Davis knew the drill and started filling the syringes with baby bird formula and got out the container of meal worms. They fed the babies together and enjoyed the quiet of the morning and the innocence of the hatchlings and fledglings.

"Harold, I do hope there is a future for the birds," he said with a speck of brightness in his voice.

Harold picked up a mealworm with tweezers, squashed its head so that it would not bite the baby bird while it was in its crop and then plopped it in the open eager squawking mouth. The sparrow swallowed and gaped for more. Harold looked intently at Davis. "Ever read any Emily Dickinson?"

"No, I prefer nonfiction and scientific journals."

"Do yourself a favor and read 'Hope' and you might have a bit more optimism."

Harold smiled as he watched Davis stick his pinky finger inside the mouth of the gaping sparrow. If he could have had a son and had a say in how that son would be, he would have made him exactly like Davis. Well, maybe not the long, blonde ponytail, but all the rest.

"Just look at him trying to gobble my finger like it's a worm," Davis said as delighted as a preschooler.

They smiled at each other and as always Harold offered a second cup of tea and just as they always did, they each had a second mug and went outside to sit on the bench and watch the sky for any traces of birds returning. The roses were in full bloom and a brilliant bush, twice the size of the others, in the back corner had branches heavy with massive, vibrant, pink blossoms.

They sat together on the bench near the bush in quiet. A closeness had formed between them during the last several months and there was no need to talk. They sipped their tea and breathed in the fragrant aromas wafted throughout the yard. Harold heard a woodpecker that sounded nearby and could hear the constant chatter coming from his bird room. It truly was a beautiful day and another chance for something wonderful to happen and life to keep moving forward.

--

It was Wednesday 10 a.m. and the weekly hour when two dear friends met for coffee. "You know you converted me to the less refined way of life don't you?" Harold said then laughed. "Coffee is for cops and blue collar workers; tea is a scientist's drink." Harold still chuckled as he added a second packet of sugar and stirred it in with the cream.

"That so? How's about I start drinking tea instead, I already read poetry," Bill said then laughed.

They spent the next few hours discussing what was being done to try and cure the humans who had been infected with the bacteria, died and turned into "stumblers" as they were known among the people. "It breaks my heart sometimes, how they are just dying slowly all over again," said Bill. "Even worse is how their families are having to make decisions about their futures because they can't think for themselves anymore."

Harold nodded in agreement. He had read reports about the killings of some of the stumblers by misinformed vigilante groups. The records were intended to be confidential, but Bill had managed to smuggle copies to him. He also knew of many cases where caretakers had opted for euthanasia rather than watch the slow, but continual deterioration. It was a pitiful predicament for everyone involved no doubt about it.

The conversation moved onto the limited efforts by the government to reintroduce birds. They both agreed that the humans came first and any natural catastrophe money the government could spare had to go to mankind.

"It's a shame about Jen and Sophie," said Stetson. "They were real sweet young ladies before, well, you know."

Harold took his time in responding. "If you think about it, the families made the right choice. They were deteriorating so rapidly and nothing like the young women they had been," Harold replied. "Sad as it is to relive the past, putting down Plato was the right thing to do and putting those girls out of their misery was too."

"Well, at least they are seeing small improvements each month with the children," Stetson said. "They may never be normal again, kind of your special needs type of kids that will never advance beyond the age of five, but they are alive."

I am not sure that is really living, especially having to eat raw meat, thought Harold, but kept his ideas to himself. He thought of the hundreds of people he was aware of who had died and knew it was a different world than it was a year ago; he had learned to look for even the smallest things to cling to in order to survive and, on some days, even feel happy.

After he finished the last drops from his mug he smiled at Stetson, a full, true smile because he was thinking of all the birds in his home waiting for his return. "I have to go there are babies that need to be fed and flowers to water." He placed a generous tip on the table and stood.

"Same time, same place next week?" asked Stetson.

Harold nodded and grinned as he headed for the door.

Chapter 15 – Migration

As California cooled and settled into winter season, Costa Rica was as hot as ever. Although Davis had just been there a week he was becoming accustomed to the early hours he had to rise at the sanctuary in order to feed the baby macaws. Living in this country so close to the equator and helping to rebuild the dwindling populations of macaws had been his dream for years. After all he had witnessed in California he felt truly mortal and knew, although he was still young, it was time to start ticking off all the biggest items on his bucket list.

He rose before the sun each day, today was no exception and staggered towards the makeshift showers for the volunteers. The chilly water was a better kick start to the day than any cup of coffee he had ever sipped. Dressed in his bathrobe, he carried his bar of soap, towel and shampoo and found his way to the showers with the help of his flashlight. Inside the small building there was a pull-string light that provided just enough light that it wasn't dangerous to step into the shower stalls.

Being the first awake, as usual, he had his choice of washing spaces and shone the light into the first stall to make sure a snake or other venomous creature was not planning to bathe with him. He turned on the water and waited for it to reach its tepid maximum before disrobing and stepping inside. With the first blast of water hitting him square in the face he was instantly awake and began a quick, brisk scrubbing and washed his hair, eager to leave the cool water as soon as possible.

He turned off the tap, wrapped his towel around his middle and shook his waist-length blonde hair as if he were a dog. Water splattered inside his stall and drizzled down his back. He was more than wide awake, he was ready to jump right into the day and savor every moment of it. His philosophy had always been "Each day has the chance for something awesome to happen" and today was no exception.

As he dressed, wrapped then rubbed his hair with the towel, he thought of the countless babies waiting in the nursery. Their sweet, pungent smell, eyes that seemed too big for their heads and the incessant squawking for food charmed him and he couldn't wait to be with them for the day. His hair was still damp, but he knew within a short amount of time the heat would dry it and it would fall into blonde waves that all the women at the complex coveted.

It was nearing dawn, but still dark enough that he needed his flashlight to assist in his return to his room. He shone the light ahead of him and went slowly. As he walked he could hear the cook setting up in the tiny kitchen and wondered what vegetarian concoction the chef had put together for him this morning. The meals were never great, but he appreciated them doing their best to accommodate his vegetarian needs.

As he strolled he began to hum the tune to "Oh What a Beautiful Morning" and smiled knowing he was making a difference in saving the macaws. As he rounded a corner in the path he saw something large in a tree branch and stopped abruptly. Fearing it was a panther he quickly shone the light at the tree. There was nothing catlike about the creature in the branch and it took him several seconds to realize it was a bird, in fact, it appeared to be the biggest vulture he had ever seen.

Final Words

I have two concerns now that the last page has been written. The first is that people will fear birds. As a human who has worked for over twenty years to help them I understand they are often misunderstood, but are usually helpful to the environment, can be loyal mates and are simply magical creatures. It is my hope that there is not a single reader who finishes the book and develops a fear of birds, rather I would hope they would learn to see them as complex creatures worthy of admiration and occasionally help. Secondly, it concerns me that as readers fall in love with Plato they might run out and purchase a parrot as a pet. Parrots live incredibly long lives, some close to 100 years. They are loud, messy and demand a lot of attention. There are thousands and thousands of parrots at bird rescue sites around the country because so many people give up on them as pets. If inspiration hits and the idea of having a parrot becomes overwhelming, research rescue groups in local areas and adopt a bird. Do not purchase one from a pet store there are so many birds that are waiting for a home and are wondering where their new flock is and how they will fit in as they actually love and feel rejection and sadness. There is an authentic group called ARA in Costa Rica that is working to rebuild the population of macaws in the area as their numbers have rapidly dwindled over the years. The sad irony is that the number of wild macaws declines while the amount of parrots in rescue shelters around the country climbs each day. Please think adoption when you consider getting a bird.

In writing this book my entire family became involved and urged me on as they waited to see what would happen to Harold, Plato and the population of California. Each person in my home made special requests for scenes to be written and begged for updates each day as I followed Harold on his journey. In particular, I need to thank my son, Ben, who read the story several times and offered keen insight and ideas. I have never been so thankful for his voracious appetite for books and his knowledge of fiction. He came up with ideas that were incorporated into some of my favorite chapters. My sister, Chris, emailed almost daily asking for more pages to read. She found herself so caught up in the journey she was an inspiration and someone I could not let down. My husband, Jeff, my other sons and daughter often asked for updates and encouraged me. My son, Davis, has helped me so much over the years in raising orphan birds I chose to honor him by actually naming a character after him. I am thankful for all the love and support and that I kept pushing forward each day until the book was finished. Sometimes it takes an entire family to write a novel.

Printed in Great Britain
by Amazon